BULLSHOT

Also by Martin Noble

Private Schulz
Ruthless People
Tin Men
Trance Mission
Bloodbath at the House of Death
One Magic Christmas
Who Framed Roger Rabbit

BULLSHOT

MARTIN NOBLE

ADAPTED FROM THE SCREENPLAY BY

ALAN SHEARMAN
RON HOUSE
AND DIZ WHITE

AESOP Modern
Oxford

AESOP Modern Fiction
An imprint of AESOP Publications
28 Abberbury Road, Oxford OX4 4ES, UK
www.aesopbooks.com

Second paperback edition published by AESOP Publications, 2015.
Copyright (c) 2015 Martin Noble, Diz White, Alan Shearman and Ron House

Publishing history
First paperback edition published by Star Books, W.H. Allen & Co. Ltd, 1983.
First hardback edition published by AESOP Publications, 2015.

Bullshot the movie was produced by HandMade Films (Productions) Ltd in 1983.
Screenplay by Ron House, Diz White and Alan Shearman,
Director: Dick Clement, Producer: Ian La Frenais, Associate Producer:
David Wimbury, Executive Producers: George Harrison and Denis O'Brien.

Special thanks to Derek Cunningham and John Neville-Andrews
for contributions to original dialogue.

The right of Martin Noble, Diz White, Alan Shearman and Ron House
to be identified as the authors of this work has been asserted in accordance with sections 77
and 78 of the Copyright Designs and Patents Act 1988.

'Bullshot' lyrics by Dick Clement, John Du Prez and Alan Shearman
Copyright (c) 1983 Ganga Publishing B.V.

With grateful acknowledgement to H.C. 'Sapper' McNeile,
the creator of 'Bulldog Drummond'.

A catalogue record of this book is available from the British Library.

ISBN: 978-1-910301-26-5

CONTENTS

PART 2   BULLSHOT CRUMMOND BOUNCES BACK

Bullshot – gosh you've done it again
You saved the human race
Bullshot – with your dazzling brain
And every hair in place!
You make the ladies' hearts go pitter patter
'Cos you're every inch a man – oh
Bullshot – yes you've done it again
As only Bullshot can.

When it seems that hope has diminished
Villains jeer and scoff
Just when everything appears finished
Bullshot pulls it off!

Bullshot – we're so terribly proud
You really saved the day
Bullshot – hear the roar of the crowd
Hop-Hip-Hip Hooray!

The hero of the Amsterdam Olympics
And British through and through
Bullshot – let us shout it aloud
We're in love with
So in love with
Madly in love with you.

PROLOGUE

The Somme, 1916

THEY WERE ALL here: all the chaps who mattered. The nucleus of the Royal Loamshire Regiment, each personally singled out for his special and unique skills by an extraordinary leader.

Most were getting a few hours' kip. 'Lofty', handsome six-foot-four fireball, ladies man but first-rate gunner; 'Handy' Alsop, mechanical wizard, soul of discretion; 'Hawkeye' McGilliecuddy, giant Scot, Hun couldn't hear him but he could see them coming; Duggie 'Lugs' Billington, ears like a rabbit, Hun couldn't see him but he could hear them coming; 'Messy' Dobbs, Captain's batman, uniform always spotless, could turn muddy blood-stained leather boots into mirrors, tarnished brass into gold, trench food into a Ritz banquet.

And then there were the regulars, the all-rounders, chaps you could rely on, with willing hearts, capable hands, and legs to follow their leader to hell and back. Men like Cunningham and Erskine ... and Dusty Miller. Salt of the earth. If the Hun didn't get them by the time this whole damn business was over, they'd be war heroes, reaping all the rewards of fame and fortune that peacetime could shower on them.

If the Hun *did* get them, they wouldn't go down without the dickens of a fight. Not if their leader had anything to do with it. The man they all hero-worshipped in the trenches, whose name sent tremors of fear across a nation's army.

'Who is this Crummond bloke?' asked Nobby Clark as he huddled in the blackness of the trenches on lookout with Cunningham and Erskine.

The two older men looked at him in stunned disbelief. He was barely out of nappies, his voice hadn't broken and he didn't need a razor. If Nobby didn't know who Bullshot was, he wouldn't last long.

As the low thud of artillery fire could be heard in the distance, the three drew closer for warmth, comfort and companionship. Nobby struck a match and the three of them crowded round the flame. For a few seconds Cunningham's rugged, athletic form, Erskine's ratty features and Nobby's smouldering eyes and baby-smooth skin were illuminated in the glow as they lit their cigarettes.

Nobby leaned down to light his and, for a brief moment that he would carry with him to his grave, he caught sight of a pair of grim, determined eyes, a lethal-looking nose in a steely face – then the wide mouth contracted as Captain Hugh Crummond blew out the flame. In the gloom the privates shuffled to attention.

'You must be new here, laddie,' Captain Crummond said sternly. 'What's your name?'

'Clark, sir. Nobby Clark.'

Crummond glanced at the three of them. 'Do either you or your two chums know the expression, "Three on a match"?'

'Heard it mentioned, sir,' Erskine replied nervously, 'but never knew the meaning.'

'Isn't it something to do with bad luck, sir?' Cunningham suggested.

'It's not a question of luck, Cunnington,' Crummond rebuked him.

'Sorry, sir,' Cunningham muttered, deciding it would be churlish to correct the mispronunciation of his name.

'In the trenches it can mean the difference between life and death,' Crummond said tersely. 'Here, let me show you.' He took the box of matches from Nobby and struck one, holding the flame aloft and out towards Erskine.

'When you light the first cigarette, the enemy sees the flame.' He held the flame out towards Cunningham. 'On the second, he takes aim—' he moved the flame to Nobby '—and on the third, he fires.'

There was a sudden deafening burst of gunshot.

'Carry on,' Crummond ordered, and walked smartly away to the officers' mess as Nobby, fatally wounded, fell to the bottom of the mud-filled trench.

The two older men looked at Nobby in stunned

disbelief. Barely out of nappies, his voice unbroken, he hadn't needed a razor.

If Nobby had known who Bullshot was, he would have lasted longer in the Loamshires.

In fact, he would have lasted.

PART 1

THE RISE
AND FALL OF
BULLSHOT
CRUMMOND

1

IN WHICH CAPTAIN CRUMMOND IS VISITED BY ENNUI AND BY LORD BINKY BRANCASTER

G OD, PEACETIME WAS tedious, mused Captain Hugh 'Bullshot' Crummond, DSO, MC & Bar, late of His Majesty's Royal Loamshires. In spite of his formidable sporting achievements and the occasional undercover assignments for His Majesty's Secret Service, Britain's most decorated hero and former number-one ace pilot had found little in recent years to satisfy his insatiable appetite for adventure in the cause of that finest of institutions – the British Empire.

As his valet and ex-batman Dobbs applied a cutthroat razor squarely along his master's manly jaw, Crummond eyed its steely reflection grimly in his shaving glass: the last time that trusty blade had seen action was in pursuit of the Bolivian Hermaphrodite across three oceans, over the lofty Himalayas and into the steamy Borneo jungle, where the little chap had buried itself dutifully into the creature's bosom, and brought an end to one of the most fiendish scoundrels the world had ever seen.

But that had been no more than an amusing diversion. Dark forces threatened the civilised world as much as its frivolous pursuit of jazz music, cocktail parties and the Charleston – and who could doubt that chief of all evils was the dreaded Hun?

Not so long ago, the elimination of the entire Teutonic

race had been the only respectable occupation for a sportsman, a gentleman and an Englishman. Now the world had gone mad and even Bullshot had allowed himself to be lured into dallying with the social flotsam and jetsam of the fashionable Mayfair and Chelsea sets.

And yet the rounds of shooting, fishing and consuming innumerable kippers in nightclubs had begun to pall, casting his fertile, restless mind longingly back to darker, more dangerous days when in the skies over France he had come face to face with his arch-enemy, Count Otto von Brunno, the abominable Black Baron of Blitzburg.

What would he now give to wipe the smile off that despicable Hun's face and get even with his foe! That would be a challenge that would stretch his ingenuity and test his courage, he thought, as Dobbs wiped the last vestiges of soap from his master's thrusting chin and retreated into the nether regions of Crummond's Mayfair chambers to prepare his breakfast.

Bullshot puffed at his pipe, savouring the powerful nicotine ambrosia of Thomas & Blather's Extra Strong Tobacco, and glanced idly at his reflection in the glass.

Not a bad picture all round. A pretty decent-looking chap stared back at him, a mere half dozen inches and a whisker below six feet in height, and broad in proportion. No one could call him handsome, but he had a kind of rugged manliness and a cheerful ugliness that inspired confidence in all but the foolhardy who would dare to cross swords with him – and who would soon learn to quake at the knees at the mere mention of his name.

As for the ladies, they seemed to melt under the steady, penetrating gaze of his eyes. The remarkably long eyelashes offset the overwhelmingly masculine effect of a mouth that was not small and which had an infectious sort of grin, a nose that had been lent a certain individuality from his final year in the Public School Welter Weights. His chest and lungs were matched for strength and stamina by his powerful stride. His heart beat at a rather low rate, even in a spot of bother. His liver and kidneys—

'Shall I grill them, guv'nor?' Dobbs called out from the kitchen.

Crummond puffed thoughtfully at his pipe.

Dressed in morning wear – red carnation, white silk shirt and blue suit, Lord Binky Brancaster was a foot taller than Hugh Crummond, but somehow less substantial, almost spectral. He draped himself like a crumpled Union Jack flag across a chair by the breakfast table and tucked in to toast and marmalade.

'Why so down, old chum?' enquired Binky of his erstwhile Eton and Oxford pal. 'You look as though you've just seen a ghost.'

Bullshot regarded him bleakly for a second. 'No fear, Binky,' he replied from his leather club chair where he was skimming through *The Times*. It was the usual mixture of tittle-tattle – 'INFLUENZA EPIDEMIC SWEEPS LONDON', 'WHO WILL WIN THE HENLEY REGATTA?', 'CAPTAIN CRUMMOND TO RIDE IN THE LONDON-TO-BRIGHTON CAR RALLY' – nothing he didn't already know, until an inconspicuous item on page 19 caught his eye:

Professor Rupert Fenton to demonstrate results of new
formula at the Royal Society of Scientific Discoverers.

He logged the article in his mind and turned back to
his friend.

'It's this damned peace I find so intolerably dull,' he
explained. 'And yet, in a way, I was reminded of a ghost
of my past this morning.'

'You've lost me old bean.'

'I'm talking of Count Otto von Brunno,' Bullshot said
darkly.

'Great dickens, Crummond!' Binky spluttered,
spilling crumbs of toast and marmalade on his dark blue
tie. 'You mean the notorious Black Baron of Blitzburg? Is
that beastly Bosch here?'

'No, thank heaven,' Crummond replied, clenching his
teeth. 'And yet, in a funny sort of way, Binky, I wish he
were, so that I would have the chance to put an end to
the Hun's machinations for good. Did I ever tell you how
I first met him?'

Binky, his mouth full of toast, shook his head.

'I remember when I first volunteered for the newly
formed Royal Flying Corps,' Bullshot began with a
faraway look in his eye. 'There were quite a few moist
eyes in the Loamshires mess-hall that day – I had already
shown myself to be something of a leader—'

'And how, Crummond,' said Binky, admiration
shining out of every pore of his blue-veined skin, ready
as always to blow the trumpet for his modest chum. 'A
born leader, I'd say. Some chaps have made a pretty
good dent in history by ordering other chaps around,
and so on, who'd still find it beastly difficult to get
through the front pages of *The Times* – take Attila the
Hun or Napoleon. Then there are other fellows who

make damn good wofflers or who can churn out a poem or some other pansyish nonsense, but couldn't tell one end of a rugger post from the other – look at Shakespeare.'

Binky buttered himself another slice of toast and went on, 'And then there are boffins who can blow up things or put them back together again – but they're mostly foreigners and certainly none of them captained England in cricket, won Wimbledon and rowed for Oxford in the same year, except you, Crummond.'

'Thanks, Binky old chap,' said Bullshot modestly. 'I soon became a decent flyer—'

'Decent!' Binky butted in again. 'You were England's top ace!'

For Hugh Crummond gratitude was mixed with exasperation at this second interruption. After all, he thought, there was only so much hero worship that a chap could take without getting too big for his boots.

'My Sopwith Camel,' he continued, 'was my faithful companion and it was not too long before the taut, shiny canvas of its fuselage was dotted with little Iron Crosses. But even up in the sky I liked to keep a friendly contact with the chaps down in the trenches: a little wave, a waggle of my wings, would do wonders for the morale of those brave, battle-weary Tommies.

'I remember the time I did a daisy-cutter. Flew so low I could even make out their little eyes peering through their hapless mud-covered faces. It certainly raised their spirits when I waggled my wings. "Look, it's Captain Crummond! Good on you sir!" one of them shouted and then they all cheered and waved madly.'

'What a story, Crummond,' said Binky, as Dobbs poured him some more coffee. 'That must have been a sight they would carry with them to their graves.'

Bullshot frowned. 'Unfortunately true, Binky. My joystick jammed and down I went. Luckily I landed butter side up.'

'And what about the Tommies?'

'Pretty nasty mess, I'm afraid. Mind you, we quickly got the old Camel up in the air again and it was soon afterwards that I first locked swords with Count Otto von Bruno.'

'What happened?' asked Binky, his knowledge of the story as hazy as his grasp of life in general...

'It was just after he shot down good old Pinky Pinksworth,' Bullshot recalled...

'A toast, sir,' said the RFC's second-best flying ace, Teddy 'Pinky' Pinksworth, DCO, MC & Bar, after being downed and taken prisoner by Count Otto von Brunno. 'You bested me, but there's one man who will be your match.'

'No doubt you mean Captain Hugh Crummond,' the Count sneered as he arrogantly smoked a Haus Bergmann cigarette through an elegant holder and poured himself a glass of champagne. 'I have a rendezvous vith ze gallant Englander at five thousand feet. It will be an honour for him to perish at ze hands of Count Otto von Brunno.' He raised the glass to the German officers assembled around him.

'And now, gentlemen, my toast: ze death of Bullshot Crummond!'

Lord Binky Brancaster buttered himself yet one more slice of toast as Bullshot carried on his story.

'It was no secret, both among the Kaiser's elite Flying Corps and among our chaps, that the odious Black Baron of Blitzburg had sworn to destroy me.

'Well, one day, in the spring of 1918, I had a hunch that the beastly Hun was in the vicinity...'

'I soon espied his Fokker D7 making a beeline for me at five thousand feet; our rendezvous was on schedule and soon I could see the whites of his evil Teutonic eyes.

'He grimaced as he lined himself up to fire on me and I could have sworn, Binky, it was the smile of the Devil himself. He managed to burst a dozen rounds into my fuselage, laughing maniacally as he fired, but it was just a graze and I quickly put the Camel into a tight loop-the-loop to come in hard on the Hun's tail.

'With deadly accuracy my SE5's Vickers machine gun tore into the flimsy fuselage of the Bosch's Fokker D7. I must admit, Binky, I allowed myself a wry smile of satisfaction before I moved in for the kill. But then a strange thing happened.'

Binky was all ears.

'I spotted that the German's machine guns had jammed and I could clearly see that the Kraut's fumbling attempts to correct the mechanism were doomed to failure.'

'You are one of a special breed, Hugh. You would not take advantage of an unarmed man.'

'Exactly, Binky. Instead of firing, I flew alongside the Black Baron's biplane to salute a worthy adversary.'

'You waggled your wings?'

'Indeed I did. Only to be greeted by an ancient Teutonic gesture.'

'The contemptible swine, Crummond. But why, then, didn't you blast him to smithereens after you saw how he repaid your courtesy?'

'It was too late, Binky. I did the decent thing, of course, and averted my gaze. By the time I had glanced back, the cowardly Hun had looped orff back to base. My act of chivalry was to have dire consequences, as you know, Binky. Although I've knocked him for six each time, the Black Baron of Blitzburg's three attempts to take over the world would never have occurred if I had finished off that Fokker in the first place.'

Binky swallowed the last of his coffee. 'What you

need, old boy, is a challenge, a change of scenery, something that will stretch your ingenuity and test your courage. Actually, I was wondering if you'd be a good egg and help me to see the pigeons off the estate.'

Another pigeon shoot. Bullshot sighed: it wasn't a patch on skewering Huns.

2

In Which Miss Fenton Stumbles on the Catalyst and Lord Binky Brancaster Stumbles on a Pigeon

As Miss Rosemary Fenton cycled her three-wheeler along the hedgerows and rose gardens of The Elms, her picturesque, but modestly cosy sixty-roomed Tudor mansion in the sleepy hamlet of Horsted Keynes, Sussex, the brilliant sunlight of a glorious June afternoon poked its nose playfully into her white, short-sleeved blouse and tweed jodhpurs, dappled in her blonde hair, sparkled in her wide blue eyes, highlighting the delicate tip of her retroussé nose and casting a warm, playful glow on her receding chin.

Perched high on the saddle she pressed her proud, perky bosom stiffly forward, pushing her behind out and up into a raised, prominent position that begged attention – and received it from her yapping corgi and from the ancient family retainer, who tugged his forelock respectfully.

Dismounting with the grace of a fledgling swan, she removed her basket from the handlebars, lifted out a bunch of freshly picked primroses, breathed their fragrance ecstatically and tripped indoors with uplifted heart.

Miss Fenton was a filly of the finest breeding, a creature of delicacy and spirit. The hard edges of the modern, material world may have been a mystery to her

– she had absorbed remarkably little from her Roedean education and her reading was now principally confined to Arthurian romance and the scandal pages of the *Illustrated London News*.

But in the area of feeling she was a veritable oil well, possessed of a fecundity of tiny, sparrow-like emotions, each perfectly distinct, constantly bewildering and absolutely indescribable. Description was, in any case, not her forte, any more than was the piano.

No, Rosemary Fenton was more like a harp, her strings itching to be plucked and twanged by a maestro of the human heart, who would modulate her sharps, fluctuate her flats and make glorious music out of the fluttering vibrations, the janglings and the tinklings in her schoolgirlish soul that nightly threw her into terrible turmoil as she dreamt of a dashing hero, a lantern-jawed Lancelot, a gal-rescuing Galahad, fighting for England, the Empire and Miss Rosemary Fenton, living for her glance, dying for a chance to defend her honour.

However, the romantic territory that was Miss Fenton had yet to be discovered, conquered and colonised. This was not because of the look and shape of the land itself – she was as sweet and delectable as an English rose, daffodil or wallflower: fair, willowy, toothsome – but, since her mother's tragic death, Rosemary had devoted herself to the care and welfare of her aged father.

In his latter years Professor Rupert Fenton had come to inhabit a role that he had once affected – that of irascible, absent-minded scientist – and now divided his time between, on the one hand, the top-secret work in which he was engaged in his laboratory and, on the other, spurning and rejecting like an ungrateful Prospero the dedicated motherings of his Miranda.

Knowledge of the aches and torments of young women held no interest for Professor Fenton – human biology was not his field, although he had made a special study of spiders. But late at night in his lab, as he fiddled with his test tubes, he would feel the dim twinges of paternal responsibility, especially when obliged to consume his daughter's home-made scones.

He was becoming convinced, although he had yet to perform the necessary clinical trials to prove his suspicions, that Rosemary's scones could well be the Hardest Substance Known to Man. He had, to date, failed to chew, let alone digest, a single one of them, and when faced with yet another plate of the wretched compounds he would wonder if his daughter was ever going to find a husband who would take her off his hands and get her out of the house.

In his ground-floor laboratory the Professor was squinting myopically at a bubbling retort through tri-focal lenses. His sight was deteriorating and vital it was at this stage in his experiments that nothing should impair his capacity to complete his work. Only he and one other scientist knew the profound implications it would have for the future of mankind. Fortunately his German rival could have no knowledge of his progress, otherwise ... His formula in Hun hands was just too abominable to contemplate.

Hastily he returned his concentration to an array of chemicals and liquids, adjusted the flame level of a Bunsen burner, and carefully poured an evil-looking yellow liquid from a test tube into a small beaker.

'Excuse me, Daddy,' tinkled Rosemary in her cut-glass voice as she floated gracefully – although possibly *waded clumsily* would have been a better description – through a sea of scientific paraphernalia, crossing to a complicated arrangement of flasks, tubes, tripods and clamps and attempted to force the rubber bung from a bell jar connected by glass tubing to a conical flask. Suddenly it flew apart, sending the tubing and flask crashing to the floor.

'Rosemary!' boomed the boffin in alarm. 'What do you think you're doing?'

'Sowwy, Daddy,' said Rosemary sweetly. 'I needed a taller vase.' Coyly she produced the primroses from behind her back.

'That's part of my experiment,' he grumbled. 'It will take me days, weeks, months, maybe years, to put this together again.'

'Don't be so cwoss,' she sighed. '*You've* been *working* much too hard!'

'Cross!' Professor Fenton exploded. 'Don't you realise the pressure I'm under? I'm on the verge of a scientific breakthrough, but I can't find the catalyst.'

'Where do you think you might have put it last?' Rosemary tried to be helpful, looking vaguely around the laboratory.

The Professor gritted his teeth. 'Rosemary, please!'

'Is it in that little dwawer where you keep your pipe?' she suggested brightly.

'If you want to further the cause of science, leave me alone and go to your room!'

Rosemary stamped her foot. 'I'm not a child, Daddy. I'm a gwown up now!'

The Professor regarded his willowy daughter despondently. 'You've been grown up far too long. It's high time you found yourself a husband.'

Silly Daddy, thought Rosemary maternally. 'I pwomised Mummy I'd always take care of you – and, golly, you need it! Look at this mess!' Briskly she began tidying up, picking up a petri dish and pouring the contents into a large glass bowl filled with a viscous chemical that formed a crucial link in the chain of his experiment.

'*Don't mix those chemicals!*' he screamed. '*That's how we lost Mummy!*'

His last words were obliterated as, with a tremendous explosion and a blinding flash, the main laboratory window was blasted into the garden. The ancient family retainer was hurled into the rhododendrons. Rosemary flitted about the room, swatting small flames with her lace handkerchief and coughing, while her father sat at his bench, head slumped in his hands.

Then, from a corner of the lab, came a faint but curious squeaking sound and, as the smoke cleared, the source became visible. A little wheel, driven by the gurgling, bubbling apparatus, had begun to turn.

'My experiment!' Professor Fenton gasped. 'It's working!' Almost like a father gazing on a daughter, he stared with something like affection at Rosemary. 'You found the catalyst,' he added in wonder.

She beamed. 'I knew it would be awound here somewhere.'

Captain Hugh Crummond, flanked by his old chum Lord Binky Brancaster and his manservant Dobbs, strode briskly and determinedly through the shadowed arches of Binky's ancestral home, Brancaster Hall, and out into the bright sunlight of the estate, a few miles from the dozy village of Horsted Keynes. The three were dressed for shooting and Bullshot was dressed to kill.

'I say, Crummond,' Binky remarked. 'Jolly decent of you to help me slaughter these beastly pigeons. This time of year they're a frightful nuisance.'

It was tough-going trying to keep up with Bullshot's masculine march and, tottering tipsily alongside him, Binky was like a man who had imbibed one gin too many and was walking home in the dark along a cliff edge. Dobbs, meanwhile, adopted the stiff gait of a private who had been given his marching orders.

'Not the same as having the Hun in your sights, is it
Dobbs?' Bullshot said cheerily to his ex-batman. 'I have
nothing against the pigeon. He poses no threat. But,
heavens, it seems like only yesterday that we were in the
trenches and had them on the run!'

'The pigeon?' asked Binky, all at sea – as indeed he
generally was about most things in life.

'No, the Germans,' Bullshot snapped impatiently. 'By
Jove, peacetime is tedious.'

They were soon in the woods on the perimeter of the
estate and, with no apparent thought or hesitation,
Bullshot swung his rifle to the sky and fired. After a
second's pause, there was a squawk, then a clump, as a
dead pigeon landed squarely at his feet.

'Nice shot, sir,' called Dobbs, transferring it to his
satchel.

But even as he spoke, Bullshot fired again, this time
without even looking, for his face was turned to Binky's
and he fired over his shoulder.

'How the dickens did you do that?' exclaimed Binky,
flabbergasted, as yet another pigeon landed between
them.

'Simple, Binky,' Bullshot replied as, with magnificent
foresight, he uncocked his rifle to demonstrate his
answer with arm movements that were stunning both in
their agility and complexity. 'By rapidly calculating the
pigeon's angle of elevation from the reflection in your
monocle and subtracting the refractive index of the lens,
I positioned myself at a complementary axis and fired.'

He recocked his rifle and marched on.

'It was no challenge at all.'

Binky was turned to frozen jelly.

3

IN WHICH THE YARD IS DAUNTED BY A FLABBERGASTING FORMULA AND FLOORED BY A DAGGER FLAUNTED IN A GARTER

THE DARKNESS of night had closed on The Elms and slowly but relentlessly the fog and mist crept over the estate, curling its tongues against the tall windows and stroking the twin towers of its chimneys – as it had for nearly four centuries. The old Tudor mansion had become a fortress against the outside world – and who could say what crimes, passions and dreams were festering in other similar fortresses, shrouded by that same billowy blanket?

Inside the house several lights were on, casting a ghostly light on two cars in the driveway: the Professor's brown and black Alvis saloon and a blue Wolseley belonging to Colonel Sir Robert Hinchcliff of Scotland Yard. In the laboratory the little wheel was spinning madly.

'Very impressive, Rupert,' said the sleek, elderly spy-catcher who, like his Marlborough and Cambridge friend, was dressed for dinner, lovingly prepared by Rosemary and mostly uneaten, not only because of the Professor's haste to reveal his important breakthrough to his closest companion, but also because it was practically inedible.

It was not for nothing that Hinchcliff had risen to preeminence in the Spy Catching Division of Scotland Yard. 'I had no idea you were working on a project of such significance,' he added. 'Have you ever told anyone about this?'

'Only a handful of colleagues at the Royal Society of Scientific Discoverers,' the Professor replied offhandedly as he made a few final adjustments.

Hinchcliff frowned. 'I wish you hadn't. This is a matter of national security. In the wrong hands this formula could unleash the dogs of war.'

The veteran Hun-hounder was deadly serious but the Professor was not impressed. 'Oh, you Scotland Yard chaps see spies behind every bush,' he replied complacently. 'What could possibly happen here in the middle of the English countryside?'

Even as Professor Fenton spoke these words, in the dark skies above the English countryside, unheard and unseen by the two eminent Englishmen, a biplane was speeding over Southern England, the noise of its engine deceitfully muffled as a result of the duplicitous manipulations of foreign mechanics.

'Otto! Where are we? We have been flying for hours!' The voice from the cabin was unmistakably female, the accent unmistakably German, the voice deep and husky, a deadly combination of all that was base, dangerous and wickedly pleasurable.

'Be quiet, Lenya! We shall be arriving soon,' came a harsh voice from the cockpit.

A moment later the engine began to splutter.

'Otto! What is ze matter with ze engine?'

'There seems to be some trouble with ze petrol – we will have to jump!'

'We cannot jump – we will be killed!'

'Don't worry, Lenya – I have thought of everything! Put on ze parachute!'

'A bodyguard, Hinchcliff?' the Professor grumbled as he retired with the Colonel into the warm living room, where a cheerfully burning fire awaited them. He seated himself in an overstuffed armchair. 'You don't mean hundreds of your charges from Scotland Yard swarming all over the house in muddy boots?'

'No, of course not,' the old sleuth replied. 'They'd be far too suspicious. No, I have in mind someone we use from time to time – off the record, you understand.'

'Who?' barked the Professor. Some eager young blockhead barging around his lab and asking idiotic questions no doubt. He sighed.

'He is called Hugh Crummond.'

From out of the starry skies two figures descended in their parachutes, like tiny marionettes falling into a toy farmyard. But these were no mere puppets, and as their biplane crashed into the undergrowth, the unwholesome German couple climbed to their feet, unstrapping their parachutes.

'Lenya! Are you alright?'

'Yes, but no thanks to you!' she muttered, throwing her parachute into a bush.

The tall, sinister Hun pulled out a roll of paper from the top pocket of his flying jacket and spread it out on the grass.

'Ze map shows that we have crash-landed in exactly the right location. Over there is ze mansion we shall be staying in, Netherington Manor, and in that direction—' he pointed '—is ze town of Horsted Keynes.'

'You mean Horsted Keynes – England?' said Lenya.

'Precisely! And that light over there is from ze home of Professor Rupert Fenton!'

'Ze famous British scientist?'

'Yes, who has just made a rather interesting discovery!'

The woman drooled with excitement and purred seductively at her partner. 'Yes, Otto! Tell me more.'

'I will explain everything as we drive to his house.'

'Drive, Otto? And exactly *how* do you propose that we drive?'

'In our new Mercedes, which is waiting for us over ... here!'

He pointed to the map, and then to a sleek black car that did indeed appear to be waiting for them a hundred yards away, its driver asleep at the wheel like some kind of hideous sloth, while a large bird of prey was perched ominously on the front passenger seat.

'Otto, you think of everything!' Lenya purred with pleasure.

'*Captain Hugh "Bullshot" Crummond?*'

Rosemary, in fetching pink taffeta, instantly turned crimson and crashed the tray of coffee cups on the sideboard.

'Did that sound like a crash to you, Fenton?' said Hinchcliff, gazing out of the window, his sleuthing instincts coming to the fore as always.

'Yes, well, I think it was rather closer to home,' the Professor sighed, looking first at the spilt milk and then at his daughter.

But at the mention of the name of a living legend, Rosemary's heart had soared like a thousand butterflies released from captivity.

'The captain of the England cwicket and polo teams?' she trilled. 'Wimbledon winner and twiple twophy holder of the London to Brighton motorcar wace?'

Hinchcliff chuckled good-humouredly. 'Yes, that's the chap. He—'

'And wasn't he the first man to conquer Kilimanjawo's southern face?'

'Yes, now—'

'And didn't he—'

'We *know* who Crummond is,' bawled the Professor impatiently. 'We all read *The Times*.'

Rosemary's face fell at the snub: in meek submission she crossed her hands.

'He's rowing at Henley this week,' said Hinchcliff gently. 'I'll have a word with him.'

Rosemary's heart beat faster. 'How *thwilling*,' she sang. 'I'd love to meet him.'

Professor Fenton had had enough of this romantic codswallop. 'Oh, go away and fetch us both a Macallan's, there's a good girl,' he sighed. With downcast eyes she obeyed.

The sleek black Mercedes-Benz sped silently along the winding tree-lined country road, its sinister headlights piercing the darkness and illuminating a signpost that read 'Horsted Keynes – 2½ miles'. The face that peered sardonically into the darkness from behind the steering wheel was eerily lit by the glow of a torch held by his voluptuous companion, who was studying the map.

'We are two minutes from ze house of Professor Rupert Fenton.'

'Within hours we shall have his formula!' replied Count Otto von Brunno – for the driver was none other than the heinous Black Baron of Blitzburg. The hideous sloth, whose name was Crouch, was now asleep in the back seat.

For an instant the orange light of a passing lamppost cast his profile into stark silhouette, the concave effect of his pointed chin and steep forehead like that of a crescent moon, his Stygian Teutonic features craters of evil as he glinted through his monocle at his slinky fur-coated mistress, the unholy Lenya von Brunno, whose very name transgressed and mocked the sacred vows of matrimony. A diabolical grin contorted the Count's menacing mouth.

'By tomorrow we will control England and in a week, ze world —'

'But, Otto,' breathed his companion in crime, fondling her pet falcon, 'Will not ze Professor be suspicious? Strange visitors in ze middle of ze night?'

'No, Lenya,' he smirked malevolently. 'We will simply tell him our car has crashed.' He rubbed his hands. 'I have thought of everything.'

'Look out, Otto!' she screamed as a sharp bend in the road appeared out of nowhere. The German's face distorted with horror. With an atrocious squeal of tyres the car skidded, ran off the road, turned a half circle and landed unceremoniously in the ditch, its wheels still spinning as they climbed out.

Lenya scowled at her fellow-conspirator. 'Did you have to make this so authentic?' she sneered.

An idea had struck the Professor. 'Is he married, this Crummond chap?' he asked the Colonel confidentially, dropping his voice.

'No, I don't think so.'

Fenton looked concerned for a moment. 'Not a pantywaister, is he?'

'Good Lord, no,' Hinchchliff said confidently. 'He's as straight as a tent pole. Bats for our team.'

Seeds of hope fertilised in the Professor's mind …

As Rosemary poured the drinks, a movement from the window caught her eye. An evil, monocled face was leering through the darkness.

'Aaaarrgghhhh!' she screamed, dropping the glass of scotch and bringing her father and Hinchcliff immediately to her side.

'What is it?' said the Professor in alarm.

Rosemary was trembling like a wet kitten.

'There's someone outside!' she shrieked.

The two men peered through the window, but all that could be seen was the malevolent, swirling mist.

'Probably your own reflection, you silly girl,' snapped the Professor, snatching the whisky bottle from his petrified offspring.

'Don't worry, my dear,' said Colonel Hinchcliff gallantly. He patted his arm reassuringly. 'I'll have a quick look on my way home.'

Outside the window, Count Otto von Brunno, Black Baron of Blitzburg, flattened his fiendish form against the wall – and waited.

Leaving the house, Colonel Hinchcliff used the light of his torch to guide the way to his car, the trained sleuth in him alert for any sign of an intruder. He stopped to examine a suspicious footprint and, moving the beam of the torch towards a clump of bushes, froze.

Illuminated by the torchlight was a shapely ankle in a stiletto-heeled shoe. Cautiously he aimed the torchbeam higher: it slowly travelled up a silk-stockinged leg, between the skit of a skirt and rested on the thigh where a jewelled dagger was thrust into a black-lace garter. A slender hand, diamond-studded fingers tipped by black-painted nails, appeared in the light of the torch and deftly removed the murderous weapon from its resting place...

4

In Which the Professor's Numbers Are Halved in a Locket and the Numb Professor Is Locked in a Harlot

AFTER THE EVENING'S excitement Rosemary Fenton was ready for her bed. She slipped into her nightgown and dressing gown, made her cocoa and flitted into the laboratory where her father was writing up his experimental notes. 'Goodnight, Daddy!' she said affectionately, lifting her cheek for a kiss.

The Professor raised his head, his eyes shining with paternal tenderness. 'Perhaps there's something in what Sir Robert says,' he declared, gazing at his brainchild still glugging and squeaking away on the bench.

Like an unripe apple dropping unwanted from a tree, Rosemary's unkissed cheek lowered itself meekly as her father took from his pocket a sheet of paper on which he had scribbled various undecipherable symbols, and tore it in half.

'Take this half of the formula and stuff it somewhere safe,' he commanded. 'If anything should happen to me, get it to the *one* man in England we can *trust*.'

Eyes fixed confidently ahead, he conjured up a mental picture of Hugh Crummond, the living embodiment of all that was great about the British Empire.

Rosemary's face had been having a busy time: anticipation, despondency, meek resignation, obedience, fear – each paid a brief visit and hastily departed, finally to be replaced with a look like melting marzipan.

'Captain Cwummond?' she gasped.

The Professor nodded proudly, strangely moved. 'He will know what to do.'

'Vewy well, Daddy,' she replied coyly. 'You can wely on me.'

Her father needed her. England needed her. Her time had come and she would not be found wanting. She turned sharply away, sensing the magnitude of the moment, and bumped into a retort with a glass tube poking from its neck. The glass shattered into tiny little fragments on the laboratory floor.

The Professor half-heartedly raised his arms, as if to will them back on to the bench. The gesture was futile. Slumping forward, he cradled his head in despair.

In her bedroom Rosemary seated herself at the dressing table and thought for a second. With quivering fingers she removed from a jewellery box a heart-shaped locket and chain – her most precious possession – and placed the formula inside. Clipping the chain around her neck, she climbed out of her dressing gown and into bed, somehow sensing that the babbling brook that was her life was about to be conjoined with a vast, powerful and surging river, whose course would lead her she knew not where …

Professor Fenton was tidying up in his laboratory when he heard rapid knocking on the front door.

'Help! Help!' came a deep, husky voice.

'Is that you, Hinchcliff?' he called gruffly.

At the door stood an alluring female in high-collared mink. 'There has been ze most *terrible* accident,' she gasped, and fainted into his arms.

'My poor child,' the Professor comforted, strangely moved as he supported her swaying body against his.

Through the mist and fog an evil presence seemed to swirl into the house. On the threshold stood Count Otto von Brunno. He sauntered into the entrance hall, an enormous Luger in his bony hand.

'Good evening, Professor Fenton,' he sneered.

'What?' exclaimed the boffin, turning round and letting go of the woman who, in any case, was freeing herself from his innocent embrace. 'How did you know my name?'

'We know many things about you, Professor,' hissed Lenya von Brunno as the she-devil locked her would-be rescuer in a vicelike grip.

'Oooh!' he piped in alarm.

'Including your recent discovery,' added von Brunno, cocking his pistol in one hand and seizing the Professor's remaining free arm with the other.

'What discovery? I told no one about the formula!' He realised what he had just said and checked himself in alarm.

'Ha! Ha! Ha! Ha!' chortled the evil Germans.

'Who are you? My friend is a policeman, you know!'

'He won't help you! But maybe this will.' Von Brunno pulled out a Luger.

'That's a Luger! But that means you're a Hun!' Fenton looked from one to the other. 'You're both Huns!'

'Ha! Ha! Ha! Ha!' they laughed again.

'You can't drag innocent people from their homes in the middle of the night!' the Professor protested. 'This is England!'

Unheeding, the Hun and his hussy continued to laugh as they pulled him backwards out of the front door of his beloved home, and into the fog and mist of an uncertain future.

With hands together, eyes closed, and only Teddy to see, Rosemary Fenton knelt at the foot of her bed to say her prayers.

'God bless Daddy and send him to bed, God bless Mummy and put back her head,' she chanted as she did every night and then, as was her wont, added the new bits. 'And God bless Colonel Hinchcliff for being such a decent bwick ...' It was hard to think of people to bless in Horsted Keynes. Then she remembered. 'And Captain Cwummond —'

Perhaps it was the sound of a heinous laugh or her father's muffled protest that distracted her. Crossing to the window, she observed, like some phantasmagoria, the chilling scene through the chink between the curtains: her father, hands raised above his head, being pushed into his own car by an evil-looking man in a black overcoat and black Homburg hat, who was holding a huge gun and by a woman who looked abominably loose and absolutely shameless.

So the face at the window had not been a figment of his imagination! She gasped with fright and clutched the locket that was hanging round her neck, too petrified to make a sound ...

'So they got you too, Hinchcliff!' whispered the Professor as he was bundled into the back of his own Alvis saloon. 'Wake up man, we're in mortal peril!'

The Colonel must have been drugged for he was uncannily still. The Professor shook him by the shoulder and then croaked with fright as Hinchcliff's corpse toppled forward, the hilt of the Countess's jewelled dagger between his bloodied shoulder blades.

'You seem tense, Professor,' remarked von Brunno sarcastically. 'Perhaps Lenya can help you to calm down.'

The German Jezebel whisked out an enormous hypodermic needle of the type used to tranquillise horses. Coldly, she jabbed the quaking egghead in the rear. He grunted, stiffened and then slumped into unconsciousness as the car drove off into the darkness.

'Daddy! Daddy! Help!' Rosemary screamed from her window as she watched her abducted father disappearing in his own car. But it was too late. At the wheel of the Alvis, the Black Baron of Blitzburg cackled malignantly. For Professor Fenton and his formula were now in the hands of the Hun.

5

In Which the Captain Crouches at Brancaster and Sniffs a Whiff of Intrigue and the Count Intrigues at Netherington and Braves a Whiff of Crouch

THE GOTHIC PILE of Netherington Manor was a cruel, foreboding haunt at the best of times, but in the dawn mist it shuddered as if possessed by some monstrous, nameless evil. Fitting it was, then, that in this unhallowed hideout sojourned the cursed Count Otto von Brunno and his scheming mistress.

Fitting too that their servant was one so loathsome as Crouch. Stunted in stature and mind, he had, as if to compensate, expanded horizontally, his grotesquely hanging, unwashed, blubber-like skin pitted with pimples, scars, open sores, bumps and festering boils.

As a result of some appalling and recurring moral turpitude he had proved an easy blackmail victim for the Hun. Their power was absolute for Crouch was mute and seemingly impotent to take revenge. Fear of exposure held him in their thrall, his natural lumpish indolence offset by apparent blind obedience to their despicable demands.

Crouch waddled and slurped through life in a stupor of gluttonous debauchery, his hideous head a receptacle for alcohol and horrible thoughts, and few but the Black Baron of Blitzburg would have cared to employ one whose mind and body wallowed in such depravity. But so perverse were the designs of the odious Hun that they seemed to derive an ungodly satisfaction from attiring this carbuncle of humanity in the apparel of an English valet. The blasphemy was compounded by Crouch himself, who sullied the uniform by day and by night with base, unspeakable acts.

This travesty of all that was British had been apprised of his master and mistress's imminent arrival and his sweating, suppurating hands were blackened with soot from his crude attempts at lighting a fire – not to warm them but to extinguish the evidence of who knows what filthy felony. Slavering at the mouth, he responded to the brutal knock at the door like a demented cur, donning a soiled pair of gloves (for even the Huns could not bear these leprous hands to be laid on them) and lurching and slobbering across the forbidding main hall to avoid their vengeful wrath from falling on his hoglike head.

The Count and his adulterous paramour swept past him into the hall, ignoring his whimper of pain as the door was slammed in his face.

'Mission accomplished,' announced von Brunno triumphantly. 'Crouch!' he barked as the verminous valet pawed at the outer vestments of his persecutors.

'Ehrrr!' he grunted.

'Before you retire we have a corpse for you to dispose of.'

Crouch drooled with excitement, his piggish eyes glittering, and dropped the Count's coat and hat by the hearth.

'Ehrrr! Errh henrrh!' He eyed the Professor hungrily.

'In ze car,' snapped Lenya.

Crouch lumbered off, eager to be about his business.

'When ze Professor has recovered we will extract ze information from him,' announced the Count to his concubine. 'No one can stop us now!'

Turning to each other, they broke into peals of evil laughter.

'Hello, what's this?' said Bullshot Crummond, climbing over a stile onto the quiet country road and stopping suddenly to examine a blade of grass. The weekend's shoot had done nothing to dispel his boredom and he had been a pigeon's feather away from taking the first plane out to Albania.

'It's a blade of grass, sir,' said Dobbs obediently.

Bullshot sniffed the air, alert in every muscle. 'Yes, but there's a smudge of petroleum on it.'

'A tractor probably passed this way,' Binky suggested.

Bullshot sighed. 'Since when have British tractors been using high octane German motor fuel?' He pointed, without looking, to the ground. 'And look! Tyre marks. Two sets.'

Binky and Dobbs looked and it was as Crummond had said.

'And footprints!' said Bullshot, the bit now firmly between his teeth. 'I'd hazard a guess that a man—' he lifted both his eyebrow and voice an octave '—and a woman transferred *two* bodies from one car to another.' He gritted his teeth, pleased but still puzzled. A piece of the jigsaw was still missing.

'Bit far-fetched, old chum,' said Binky. Actually he hadn't a clue what Hugh was on about.

'Perhaps, Binky. But the metric depth confirms that

one car *was* German …'

'Gosh!' said Binky, dazzled by his friend's brilliant deductive powers. But Hugh Crummond was already further along the trail. He stooped again to pick up another object. Dobbs was unable to see it because he was looking the other way. Nor could Binky because he was as blind as a bat.

'… And this headlamp filament,' concluded Captain Crummond triumphantly, 'tells me that the other was a British saloon car.'

'Bravo, Captain,' applauded the loyal manservant. 'A brown and black Alvis it was.'

'How do you work that out, Dobbs?' said Bullshot benevolently.

'It's in the ditch, sir.'

6

In Which an Exercise Is Remembered and a Member Is Re-exercised

WITH ONLY TEDDY to comfort her, Rosemary tossed and turned all night, wondering who Daddy's abductors were, what they wanted with him, and if they knew how he liked his egg boiled in the morning. At least, she consoled herself, when they found out how grumpy he could be if the white was too runny, they would wish they'd left him alone to get on with his silly old experiments.

I wonder if Daddy's expewiment has anything to do with him being kidnapped? she thought suddenly.

Excited at her clever detective work, she tried to remember if anything unusual had happened lately. Could it have anything to do with the pile of her home-made scones that she'd found hidden in the linen basket? Then there was that little explosion the day before in the laboratory when she'd found his catalogue. And the way he'd looked so fine and British when he'd given her the piece of paper with the squiggles on it and said, *If anything should happen to me, get it to the one man in England we can trust.*

Of course! It must have something to do with Daddy's formula. *And she had the other half in her locket!* She must write at once to Captain Crummond. He would know what to do if anyone did. He was the one man

who would be able to save his father – and England –
from ... *what?* She didn't have a clue, but it must be
something pretty big if it involved Hugh Crummond.
Would he be as dashing as he looked in his
photographs? Would she melt under the steady,
penetrating gaze of his eyes?

She blushed and, seating herself at her writing
bureau, pulled out a sheet of pretty pink notepaper and
with shaky hands began to write:

My dear Captain Crummond
I am in terrible trouble and need your help desperately...

The blackened bricks and mortar that groaned beneath
the wretched curse that was Netherington Manor
shrieked out a warning to those who would venture into
its shadow. A careless laundryman had passed that way
and his wicker baskets now sat in the cellar, their
purpose yet obscure. Of the laundryman himself there
was no sign.

On this fearful day the milkman's frightened nag
reared and whinnied to be gone; gingerly the tradesman
set two pints at the foot of the immense oaken doors, and
staggered back with fright and disgust as Crouch
shuffled out, breathing fumes of whisky and something
worse. He held out three putrid fingers and the milkman
nodded nervously, returning in a moment with another
pint.

As he did so, a bloodcurdling scream rent the bowels
of the Manor, sending shivers of fear down the

tradesman's back.

Crouch giggled noiselessly.

'*My father, Professor Fenton, has been kidnapped,*' Captain Crummond read aloud at the breakfast table of his Mayfair living room.

Bullshot's kipper remained uneaten on his breakfast plate. Like a sentry patiently on duty in the trenches it kept its position faithfully between its two comrades, triangular slices of thinly cut, golden buttered, fresh white bread. Meanwhile the letter's recipient stood dramatically in vibrant maroon Chinese silk pyjamas, exquisite Persian blue silk dressing gown and imperial Indian carpet slippers, with one foot on his chair, smoking his pipe and presenting – it has to be said – a striking pose to his chum Lord Binky Brancaster.

'That must be old Rupert Fenton, the world-famous scientist,' said Binky between mouthfuls of kipper. 'We're almost neighbours.'

'Another kipper, your Lordship?' enquired Dobbs of Binky, who nodded eagerly: he had already got three down him and was game for a fourth.

'*I'm leaving for London today and will be staying at St Ermine's Hotel.*' As Bullshot read the letter, he strolled across to the polished marble mantelpiece and leaned casually against it.

Framed by the masculine military memorabilia, Crummond was the prized centrepiece, the walking trophy of his own prowess, lending the room a more imposing air than the most exclusive of gentlemen's clubs. He reseated himself in a leather chair and crossed his legs, revealing a pair of striking black gaiters below the silk dressing gown.

'*Could I see you at once?*' he finished the letter and sniffed. 'Hmm. Perfume ... shaky handwriting—' he jumped out of his seat again, like a knight from his horse '—a damsel in distress!'

'Another case, guv'nor?' enquired Dobbs from the other room.

'Too early to say, Dobbs ... and yet ...'

He held the latter up to the light. 'Family crest watermark!' His eyes narrowed as he read '"*In Libris Fentonium Sempere Sum*" – in Liberty I Am Always Fenton! Fenton! ... Now there was a Willy Fenton who served under me in France. and he used to write to his cousin – a girl whose name, if I'm not mistaken, was Rosemary! Must be her! But I wonder what the deuced sort of trouble she'd be in.'

In a pensive pose reminiscent of the late Monsieur Auguste Rodin's *The Thinker* – but with a noble English refinement that no mere Frenchman could have hope to portray – Bullshot leaned his elbow against the mantelpiece. Binky meanwhile took advantage of his chum's brief sojourn into the land of deep thought to slip off to the gentleman's room as he had drunk a rather large amount of tea.

'This gal's address is *dangerously* close to where we found the crashed motor car...' said Bullshot. He shook his head and began to pace the room, one arm pinned behind his back like a general reviewing the state of battle. Then he stopped and cocked his ear.

'But wait a minute. I can hear something. Some bounder's intruding. A marauder! It could all be connected.'

He tripped over a chair, knocking over the teapot as he ran out of the living room, and returned a moment later with Binky, whose arm he was holding in a vicelike half nelson.

'Alright, matey! Who sent you!'

'Crummond!' Binky protested. 'Have you gone barmy! It's me, your old chum Binky Brancaster. If you recall, dear fellow, we're due at Ascot at precisely 11.30 this morning.'

'And then there's 'Enley, sir,' Dobbs reminded his master.

'Ascot and Henley may have to wait!'

'Crummond!' and 'Sir!' said Binky and Dobbs in shocked unison.

'Well, dash it all, when there's a damsel in distress, a chap has to do the right thing. Anyway, Binky, what happened to you?'

'Well, if you must know, I was obliged to relieve myself, but now I think I need a quick pick me up.'

Lord Brancaster walked over to the drinks trolley and poured himself a scotch.

'There's been a pretty strange course of events this morning, Binky! Petroleum on the grass, an intruder – and then there's this letter.'

'What letter?' said Binky, who as usual was having difficulty keeping up.

'The letter I received this morning. The letter I've been reading to you. Dash it, Binky, try to keep up! *This* letter.'

He walked over to the breakfast table to pick up the letter but it had disappeared.

'Well, it seems to have gone, but look!' He picked up the teapot from the carpet and whipped out a table napkin on which was printed a near perfect transfer of the letter. 'Fortunately for us, the writing has been imprinted on this serviette!'

He handed the napkin to Binky and picked up *The Times*, which he proceeded to sit and read as Binky once more attempted to grapple with the contents of Rosemary's letter.

'"*My dear Captain Crummond, I am in terrible trouble and need your help desperately...*" Rather familiar, don't you think, Crummond? Ever met this filly?'

'Met her?' Bullshot looked up. 'No, not that I am aware of. Yet I feel I've known her since the dawn of time.'

With that he returned to the news columns of *The Times*.

'"*My father, Professor Fenton, has been kidnapped, following a mysterious airplane crash...*"'

'What's that?' Bullshot jumped up from his seat and rushed over to Binky. '"*Mysterious airplane crash!?*"' He pointed to the newspaper. '"Mysterious Airplane Crash! German aircraft found abandoned in meadow." Mmmm! You know what this means, don't you, Binky!'

'A Bosch Plot!'

'Exactly! And that can only mean one thing. It's too much of a *mad* coincidence! These *random* clues all point to one man.'

'Who?' asked Binky.

Hugh Crummond's eyes narrowed dangerously.

'Captain Otto von Brunno!'

'Streuth!' exclaimed Dobbs.

'Good Lord!' Binky chimed in. 'The Black Baron of Blitzburg!' He started to take off his jacket.

'What are you doing, Binky?'

Binky stood to attention, as if someone had struck up the National Anthem.

'Well, I can't just nip off to Ascot, Crummond – if England needs me!'

'Top hole, Binky.' Bullshot shook his hand, beaming. 'Splendid!'

'Well, what are we going to do?'

For a moment, Crummond was foxed. 'Er, well … what would you do?'

'Well, I'd form a plan of attack,' said Binky, remembering his spell in the War Office (although in truth he spent most of his time in Whitehall during the First World War as a Reserve Codebreaker; his daily duties principally being to help solve *The Times* crossword).

'No, Binky! Use your military training!' Bullshot was on the move again, as he paced the living room. 'We'll formulate a strategical offensive!' For the next few seconds he was wrapped in deep thought. 'Now you pretend to be von Brunno. Sit here—' he pointed to the breakfast table on which Binky seated himself awkwardly.

'Now, here's the girl—' he picked up the chair and placed it underneath the table '—inextricably caught up inside. Now I shall come in and attack you – and rescue the girl!' He turned and walked a few steps away and then turned again and marched aggressively towards Binky.

'Alright, von Brunno! The game's up!' They now stood face to face. 'And if it's fisticuffs you want – then I'm your bloke.' He adopted the pose of a champion boxer, fists raised menacingly. In retaliation, Binky pointed an imaginary gun in his face. 'What's that, Binky?'

'It's a gun, Crummond.'

'A gun, eh?' He looked down at his fists, realising

that they weren't quite up to the job. 'A gun? Alright!'
He raised his hands in surrender. 'Now listen here, von
Brunno, you may have me this time, I will admit it. But
there is just one small thing you seem to have forgotten!'

He leaned over backwards and pretended to grab the
imaginary gun from Binky's hand.

'Oh, what's that?' Binky said in surprise as Bullshot
dived for the gun and jumped back holding it. Unaware
of the fact, Binky continued to point his gun-fingers at
his chum.

'*I've* got the gun now, Binky,' Bullshot sighed in
exasperation. 'Alright, von Brunno! Move one muscle
and you're a dead man!'

'Oh, you won't really shoot me, will you,
Crummond?' Binky said, feigning the kind of abject
terror that was only to be expected of a cowardly Hun.

'I might, von Brunno, I just might, you sissy!' He
grabbed the chair from under the table and pulled it
away. 'And there you are, you see! I grab the girl and
make my escape!'

He replaced the chair and once more posed with one
foot on it. 'Well, do you think it'll work?'

'No.'

'It's foolproof, Binky!'

'Oh come, come, old fruit, he'd recognise you
running away, wouldn't he?'

'Recognise me?'

'Well, of course he would!' said Binky, returning to
the drinks trolley for a refill.

'Mmmm! Recognise me, eh? Well then – I'd need a
disguise.'

'Yes, and the speed of an athlete!'

Bullshot thought about this. 'Of course! I would need
the speed of an athlete. Help yourself to a beer, old chap.

Oh, if you see any athletes passing, give me a shout, will you.' He disappeared into his bedroom.

'You know I'm not a beer man, Crummond. Whisky and champers only, that's me.' Binky picked up *The Times* and turned to the racing pages as he helped himself to another slice of toast from the silver rack. 'I wonder if the King's horse is running today. I might put a guinea on it.'

As he spoke Bullshot came back into the room, dressed in long johns that displayed every inch of his athletic build and proceeded to execute Jumping Jackets.

'I say, young fellow,' said Binky, idly looking up. 'Captain Crummond must be expecting you?'

'Oh, is he indeed, really?' Bullshot replied, disguising his voice with his usual magnificent subtlety and guile. 'Well, perhaps you'd tell him I'm here.'

'If you say so,' Binky nodded and shouted across to the bedroom, 'Crummond! There's some kind of athlete here to see you.'

'Binky!' Crummond shouted back, cleverly managing to throw his voice so that it seemed to come from the bedroom.

'Where are you, old bean?'

'Binky, it's me!' Bullshot repeated, now in his normal voice.

Binky gasped. 'Oh, it's you, Crummond! Great japes, old banana, I didn't recognise you. Jolly clever,' he giggled, then he stared at his old chum, riveted by the spectacle, his half-eaten toast remaining frozen a mere lick away from his mouth, like a snapshot.

In a pose that many a Greek god would have given their right arm for, the man stood robeless, his white long johns revealing the thing that made Hugh Crummond – and Great Britain – truly outstanding.

'You haven't seen me looking like this in a while, have you, Binky?'

The Earl of Brancaster gaped. 'Er ... no, I can't say that I have ... actually.'

'Between you and me,' declared Bullshot, hands on hips as he turned the full magnificence of his frontal musculature towards Binky, 'I have a feeling something very ... big is coming up.'

'Jolly good disguise,' Binky muttered for want of anything else to say.

'Thanks,' said Bullshot, sitting down in his leather armchair with his legs wide apart. 'You know, you're a terrific boost to my confidence. People may call you an idiot and an imbecile – but as far as I'm concerned, you're my kind of nincompoop.'

Binky looked confused. 'Oh, that's good ... is it?' He went over once more to the drinks trolley. 'Any shampoo, Crummond?'

'A chap doesn't need shampoo, Binky. That kind of thing's strictly for the girls. Carbolic and Brilliantine will do fine for a chap like me.'

'Sorry, old bean, I meant shampers ... champagne.'

'Not a good idea on the hair, Binky. Messes it up and makes it unbrushable. That reminds me – I want you to pretend you're a girl.'

'Oh, I couldn't, Crummond. I haven't got the things – you know, the bits and bobs.'

'No, Binky, the girl I'm meeting at St Ermine's this afternoon. Now come along, sit you down.'

Binky did what he was told, albeit a little reluctantly and sheepishly, and sat down on the chair.

'I shall enter,' Bullshot went on, 'and attract your attention in some manner.' He glanced at Binky and then did a double-take.

'Excuse me, Madam! Are you awaiting Captain Hugh Crummond?'

'Not with you, Crummond. You're already here.'

'No, Binky, you're *the girl*.'

'Oh I see, yes, of course. Er ... I am actually,' Binky said, now in a falsetto. 'Are you he?'

'Binky, you're completely hopeless as a girl. I suppose I'll have to make do with the real thing. Dobbs, get cracking. Telephone Miss Fenton and say that I'll see her this afternoon.'

'Oh, but sir,' Dobbs reminded him, 'as I told you, we've got the 'Enley Regatta today, sir.'

Bullshot Crummond paused and raised an eyebrow. 'Dash it, you're right.' He deliberated for a second. 'I'll row a little faster,' he decided with a jaunty little nod of the head. 'A quick wash and brush up and I'll see her for tea there at four.'

As Dobbs headed for the telephone, Binky wiped the remains of toast, kipper and scotch off his mouth with a serviette. 'But what about Ascot? And I thought we were going to practise for the London to Brighton,' he said peevishly.

'That'll have to wait.'

Binky grinned. 'Nothing like a whiff of intrigue to raise your spirits, old chum.'

'Absolutely,' Bullshot agreed, adjusting his long johns in preparation for the busy afternoon ahead.

7

In Which the Black Baron of Blitzburg Breakfasts on a Bobby on His Beat, Lunches on a Knuckle Sandwich and Dines on a Bullet Burger

'BLACK BARON to Iron Fish ... over.'

'What is ze problem?' Lenya von Brunno, with her pet falcon Fritz perched on her shoulder, demanded as the Count sat over a radio.

'I cannot make contact with ze submarine. This is impossible! ... Black Baron to Iron Fish ... come in ... Aah! I have made contact! Kapitan Hauptmann! This is Count von Brunno. I am pleased to report that we have captured ze British Professor Rupert Fenton and will rendezvous at 0300 hours as arranged ... Good ... Over and out!'

He looked up. 'Well, Lenya, everything is working out beautifully. Now nothing can interfere with my plans for conquest of ze whole world.'

'Otto,' Lenya hissed as she peered out of the window. 'There is someone outside ze window! Hide ze radio while I turn out ze lights!'

A moment later there was a knock on the door.

'Respond to ze auditory stimulus, Crouch,' ordered the Count, snapping his fingers.

'Errrrr...' replied the menial. Instantly aroused by the

signal, and, like Dr Pavlov's dog, he slouched across to open the huge, oaken door. As it creaked open, all four inhabitants of Netherington, including Fritz, were momentarily dazzled by the flashlight of a uniformed policeman.

'Can I help you?' said the Count.

PC Penfold slapped his hand on his chest. 'Ooh, you gave me quite a turn. Sorry to disturb you, sir. We've had reports of radio signals being transmitted to a German submarine from this area.'

'What? Here on ze British coast? Euggh!' von Brunno gasped in what he judged with Teutonic precision to be the exact sound of Anglo Saxon lily-liveredness.

'I'm afraid so, sir. Looks like spoys.'

'*Spoys?*'

'Yes! Spoys – secret agents. You didn't happen to see any foreign-looking types pass this way, did you?'

'Ah, ze spies! No, I have seen no one.'

The constable took off his helmet and scratched his head. 'Well, don't worry sir. I'm sure we'll have them by the morning.'

The Count stifled a yawn ostentatiously.

'Oh I must have got you out of bed,' said the constable. 'I'm so sorry ... Well, goodnight.'

'*Gute nacht*,' said von Brunno, clicking his heels.

'Oh, one more thing, sir...'

'Yes?' the Count said, surreptitiously removing the Luger from his pocket.

'If you do happen to see any spies passing this way, don't try and apprehend them – they may be armed.'

'I'm sure they are, constable ... but thanks for warning me.'

PC Penfold smiled benignly. 'That's what we're here for, sir. Good night.'

'Crouch!' von Brunno clapped his hands. 'Ze door!'

Once more the minion oozed his fat, sluglike body towards the front door to release the constable from Netherington's clutches.

'You see how easy it is to deal with ze British police,' the Count remarked to Lenya once Crouch had closed the door and returned to whatever foul lair he had now come to infest.

Lenya snorted. 'If you hadn't dealt with them, Fritz would have – wouldn't you, my little one?'

'I despise that falcon! Why do you insist on keeping him here. One of these days I will fricassée that falcon!'

'He has his uses! Besides,' she added, looking at the Count's bald head, 'he is *young!* Come along, Fritz, I have a nice little mouse for you to eat.'

All was quiet in Netherington's grand hall and library. Only the howling wind and the rain that beat against the sullen window panes disturbed the still of the evening, and as the minutes went by, the Count allowed himself to savour a measure of satisfaction that so far everything was going according to plan. He was starting to dose in his armchair, when he sensed a presence behind him.

'Ah, Professor Fenton!'

He stared at the revolver that was clutched tightly in the professor's trembling hand.

'Yes!' Fenton replied with the smugness of a boffin whose experiment has succeeded.

'How did you escape from ze cellar?'

'Never mind! So, you thought you'd be taking me to Germany, did you?'

'Don't do anything foolish, Professor!'

'Don't worry about that.'

'Ah, Lenya!' said the Count, raising his hand as she quietly entered the library.

'Huh!' scoffed the Professor. 'You don't think I'd fall for an old trick like that! Why, during the war ... You fiends!' he added as Lenya grabbed the gun from his hand.

'Professor! We have changed our plans. You must complete your process in forty-eight hours.'

'But that's impossible! The hardening procedure takes at least three days! Besides, you may have my formula, but you still have no idea what to do with it.'

'We shall see about that. You will hasten ze procedure! If only to save your daughter's life!'

'What? No! Leave my daughter out of this!' He fell to his knees, beating von Brunno's chest, but the Count simply knocked him to the floor.

'How long will it take us to reach Germany?' said Lenya as Fenton ran at her. With a flick of her wrist she threw him into a backward somersault and onto the floor on his back.

'That rather depends,' the Count replied as Fenton renewed his efforts and ran at him. With a flick of his foot he dispatched Fenton onto the floor, this time in a forward somersault.

'On what, Otto?'

'Obviously, ze British Navy.'

'This will never work!' she said sceptically.

'It's foolproof!'

'It seems escape is impossible!' Fenton sighed as he lay on the floor below them.

'Anxious to begin ze work, Professor?' The Count twisted the elderly boffin's arm behind his back and snapped his fingers for Crouch, who took over the strenuous task of dragging the boffin back down the stairs to the cellar.

'Otto, this whole scheme is ludicrous!' Lenya said when he returned to the library. 'I want to go back to Berlin! I want to go to my favourite nightclub. I want ze cabaret. I want to gaze at ze young blond men. I want to wear furs... I want to wear diamonds.'

'Like this one, Lenya?' said the Count, producing an enormous, glittering diamond from his pocket.

'Otto! Where did you get such a beautiful diamond?'

'They were not so difficult ... to *manufacture*!'

'Manufacture?'

'Yes, Lenya! Although flawless in every way – they are synthetic!'

'Synthetic?'

'They cost two shilling ninepenny Englishman money.'

'Ah, it all begins to make sense!'

'With these jewels we will be able to ruin ze international diamond market.'

'Thus causing ze mass unemployment!'

'Starvation!'

'Hunger!'

'Poverty!'

'And death! Death to thousands of innocent people. They will all die!' She moved towards him. 'Oh, Otto! I'm so happy! When can we begin?'

He hesitated. 'There are some formalities.'

'What formalities?' She looked at him suspiciously.

'We have still to find out about this formula of Professor Fenton's. Sure, with ze diamonds we can destroy ze world – but now we have ze formula I am thinking we can do the same thing – *and much more quickly!*'

'Otto, *mein Liebchen*,' Lenya purred with pleasure and anticipation.

'But there is just one problem. Crummond is on to us!'

'Aah! That handsome Englishman?'

'Yes, Lenya. I notice you find him ... *attractive!*'

'Well ... he is young!'

Von Brunno ran his hand over his bald head. 'Yes, and also very foolish!'

'He has foiled your plans more than once.'

'He was lucky.'

'On three occasions.'

'Baah!'

Lenya sidled up to her husband. 'Why not let me deal with Captain Crummond?'

'No, Lenya!'

'Why not?'

'On our last encounter, your fondness for Captain Crummond cost our organisation a mere 250 million lire.'

'And worth every penny!'

'I have therefore hired ze most unscrupulous gangster in America to eliminate Captain Crummond.'

Lenya gasped. '... Not ... Salvatore Scalicio!'

'Precisely!'

'Why are you using that maniac?'

'His methods have proved rather effective, don't you agree? He is due to arrive any moment and when he does, you will please attend him. Meanwhile I will put our little gem under lock and key.'

He took the diamond back from Lenya and left her alone in the library.

'So, Otto!' she muttered to herself. 'I am not to deal with Captain Crummond? Is that what you think? Well, remember, ze double-edged sword of fate has more than one side!'

Salvatore Scalicio arrived at Netherington minutes later, a huge Havana cigar clamped to his ghastly American lips, whose oiliness and thickness betrayed their Mediterranean origin. With his odious demeanour and bar-room apparel he was evidently a low-life spiv and mobster of a peculiarly base and foreign kind and thus it was hardly surprising that Crouch grovelled at his feet before showing him into the library.

Scalicio was indeed one of the most ruthless, certainly the most unkempt, criminals the New World had so far managed to produce – more vicious, it was said, than his erstwhile colleagues from the Windy City, Mr A. Capone and Mr J. Dillinger; his skills in the gun department more lethal than those of Mr B. the Kid; and when it came to cleaning the streets of ladies of the night, almost in the same league as Mr J. the Ripper – although obviously as he was not British he was never going to be a match for one of our own chaps.

'I'm Salvatore Scalicio from Chicago,' he introduced himself to Lenya.

'I'm Lenya von Brunno from Berlin,' she replied.

'How ya doin'. I'm lookin' for a guy called Bruno.'

'Well, come this way, Herr ... er ... Scalicio. Otto!' she called.

The Count immediately appeared at the door of the library.

'My ... father ... Count Otto von Brunno.'

'How ya doin', Bruno,' Scalicio drawled.

'How do you do, Herr Scalicio. As I told you, I have a little task for you to perform. But being a man of international finance, I always believe in discussing terms first. Which reminds me – there is a little something I wish to show you.'

He disappeared and returned a minute later with the 'diamond'.

'Hey, that's a real swell rock, Bruno. Must be worth a lot of dough.'

'Actually, it's worth—' Lenya began.

'Don't tell me!' Scalicio interrupted. 'It's worth 250 Gs, right?'

'You're so clever!' Lenya sneered. 'How did you guess?'

'Well, you see, I know a lot about sparklers. Hey, but wait a minute! Why are you payin' so much for only one rub-out? There must be some kind of catch.'

'There is no catch, Herr Scalicio,' Lenya assured him with a smile.

'As I explained,' said the Count, 'there is only one

man standing between me and a whole roomful of diamonds.'

'And we want him eliminated!' Lenya added.

'Well, that ain't gonna be no problem.'

'What methods do you propose to use?'

Scalicio took a puff of his cigar. 'Well, for this job, I'd go for the cement overcoat.'

'It sounds rather crude to me.'

'I ain't never had no complaints – who's the guy?'

'Oh, just one Englishman – a Captain Crummond.'

'Captain Crummond? He'll be a pushover.'

But a moment later the awesome truth sunk into Scalicio's thick Italian-American gangster skull.

'Hang on – wait a minute. You don't mean "Bullshot" Crummond, do you?'

'Do I detect a hint of ze yellow in your voice, Herr

Scalicio?' said the Count.

Scalicio glared at the German. 'You callin' me a coward, Bruno? I ain't no coward.'

'How do they say ... "as yellow as a canary"?'

The mobster screwed up his face in anger. 'Listen, Bruno. How would you like a knuckle sandwich?'

With that he tossed away his cigar and delivered an unsportsmanlike American-style punch into the lower part of the Hun's anatomy, clearly flouting the Rules formulated by the Ninth Marquess of Queensberry. For a start, the bounder wasn't wearing gloves.

Von Brunno fell sprawling to the ground and Scalicio stood over him, preparing to finish him off, and therefore breaching Rule Four specifically stating that he should have retired to his corner. But a moment before he landed the killer punch, the cheating Bosch pulled a Luger from the pocket of his dressing gown.

'You have just committed a very grave error, Herr Scalicio, which you shall now pay for – with your life!'

Scalicio's eyes widened in terror. 'Now wait a minute, Bruno ... er ... Mr Bruno ... I can explain—'

But it was too late. Tit for tat, as it were, the Count shot Salicio twice in the same portion of his anatomy as the gangster had delivered his low blow and then, adding insult to injury, spat tastelessly on his dead body and laughed.

Strangely stirred by her husband's ruthless demonstration of German supremacy, Lenya coiled herself seductively around him.

'Now that you have killed him, shall *I* entice Captain Crummond from his lair?'

'No, Lenya, that will not be necessary!'

'Why not?'

'You see, Captain Crummond will not be leaving his

lair … alive!'

'Ha! Ha! Ha!' they both laughed like hyenas.

The Count suddenly stopped laughing and adjusted his monocle.

'It is late,' he announced. 'Let us sleep. In ze morning, ze Professor will finally reveal how we can apply ze formula!'

8

IN WHICH THE PROFESSOR IS BETRAYED BY AN INVOLUNTARY SLIP OF THE TONGUE

BENEATH THE VAST cobwebbed stone of Netherington's satanic cellars came the rumbling of cart wheels. Lying prostrate and bound to a gurney was Professor Rupert Fenton, still grumbling about his morning egg, which had been as raw and runny as his nerves, but still defiant as Crouch dragged him across the cellar bowels of the building.

'Ah! Good morning, Professor!' sneered the Black Baron of Blitzburg with false bonhomie as he descended the stairs, his arm linked in Lenya's like a couple of cobras. 'I trust you slept well?'

'I'll never tell you anything!' declared the Professor bravely.

'Those who have resisted in ze past have learnt to regret their obstinacy,' hissed the Countess as they led their captive into the hub of their operations.

'Being a man of science, Professor, I think you will appreciate this little device of mine.' Von Brunno, pointing towards a fiendishly sinister-looking machine that appeared to be driven by a combination of alcohol, opium, steam, clockwork, electricity and peanut butter. 'It is designed to produce Involuntary Lingual Slippage.'

Nor indeed could the scientist in Fenton resist the seductive allure of Applied Electricity. 'Good Lord!' he cried excitedly as Lenya unslipped the knot that bound him to the gurney. Jumping up, he seated himself in a sort of dentist's chair, above which hung a helmet of steel rings. 'You've crossed the negative polarised rheostat with a four-phase carbon inductor—' He swallowed nervously. 'It could kill me...'

'That is a risk we are prepared to take,' purred Lenya, shamelessly running her fingers over the Professor's dishevelled hair and cheek. To his consternation the helmet was lowered over his head.

'You see, Professor, without your cooperation ze formula is useless.'

'Initiate maximum voltage output,' Lenya commanded.

'Affirmative,' the Count snapped as he and Crouch pushed and pulled, turned and switched various knobs, levers and buttons.

'Increase gyroscopic control.'

'Affirmative.'

'Prepare for Involuntary Lingual Slippage.'

'Affirmative.'

A little puff of steam belched from one of the machines and the Professor gurgled.

'I hope this thing's earthed,' he croaked as a small panel that read 'DANGER! INVOLUNTARY LINGUAL SLIPPAGE' started to flash on and off.

'Professor,' commanded the Countess. 'We need your help!'

'No! No!' Fenton protested fearlessly. 'I'll never tell you that half of the formula is missing—' He covered his mouth guiltily. 'Damn! What made me say that?'

'An involuntary slippage of ze tongue,' Lenya explained, as to a child. 'It's working!' she hissed to von Brunno.

'So there is more to this formula,' he hissed back to her.

More steam belched from the machine.

'Professor, we already know who has it,' declared Lenya.

'No, no, you don't!' the Professor exclaimed confidently. 'My daughter Rosemary's got it... Whoops! I've done it again.'

'And where is your beloved Rosemary hiding it?' Lenya enquired archly.

'She's not my beloved Rosemary. She's a pain in the— aaghhhh!' Steam was now pouring freely from the helmet. 'What is the matter with me?' the Professor added in astonishment.

Von Brunno was growing impatient. 'I must go to ze house and seize his daughter,' he announced to Lenya.

'There's no point – you're married already,' slipped the Professor involuntarily. 'Anyway, she won't be there if she's got any sense,' he added in a strangulated voice; he was now nearly hidden by billowing steam. 'She'll be ... be ... at ... at ... at ... at...!' The machine was starting to overload.

'His alpha waves are regressing!' Lenya shouted out over the general din.

'She'll be where?' persisted the Count.

'Henley Regatta!' spluttered the Professor involuntarily just before he collapsed and, with a dazzling flash, the devious little machine exploded.

9

In Which the Battle Is Won by an Oar and Lost by a Potted Palm

T IS A TOSS-UP whether God has created the Universe in order to stage the Henley Regatta or whether Henley has been added on afterwards – perhaps on the eighth day – as the cherry on the cake.

Maybe it amounts to the same thing and anyway who cares on this magical summer day when everyone and everything – the crowds who line the bank of the Thames and sit in marquees erected on the law in front of the Clubhouse and lounge on gaily painted verandas: fashionable ladies in pretty dresses waving their parasols, debonair young men sporting striped blazers and boaters, parties picnicking in punts, spectators sipping champagne and eating strawberries, young chaps playing banjos and guitars, and debs prancing to the latest foxtrot, tango and jazz music – all seem to have been choreographed to dance to some divine English harmony whose source is in the sparkling water and in the bluer than blue sky...

And look, here is Rosemary, transformed amazingly into a white swan, a pearl, a vision of purity in white with a large white floppy hat and a white polka-dotted cotton dress and white-lace gloves and a white parasol – and a whitish face, for Rosemary is not so much nervous as bordering on a fit of hysteria. Impervious to the glory of the occasion she has been plunged into purgatory, caught in limbo between the two men in her life – her beloved father who is in mortal danger, and the man she is about to meet, the one man who can save him.

Suddenly a shout goes up and the crowd turns its attention to the river. Between the boaters and parasols she can make out a rowing eight moving downstream. Their oars dip and turn in the brilliant, sparkling water as, through a shiny megaphone, their cox urges them on. Then another boat comes into view.

To Rosemary's amazement, and that of the crowd which begins to buzz with excitement, she sees only one man rowing. Intrigued, she hastily moves to the front of the crowd to get a better view. She gapes and involuntarily her white-gloved hand flutters to her breast.

The lone rower is Captain Hugh 'Bullshot' Crummond.

On a punt a few yards away Lord Binky Brancaster sits picnicking with three beautiful and well-bred ladies.

'Where's the rest of Captain Crummond's crew?' asks Lady Cathleen Hughes-Rotheaton.

'Influenza, every man jack of them,' Binky replies, munching contentedly on a cucumber sandwich.

'What rotten luck,' remarks Lady Sarah Wartlesby.

'The race isn't over yet,' says Binky, who knows just how hard his old chum can dip his oar in.

With mounting excitement Rosemary watches as Captain Crummond, spurred on by his manservant Dobbs at the megaphone, seems with remarkably little effort to be gaining on his eight competitors. The strength and power of the man are superhuman. He moves like a well-oiled machine, his back stiff as a ramrod, his short but powerful thighs moving in perfect coordination with his muscular arms. It is a miracle to observe.

The crowd is growing frantic with suspense as Hugh Crummond, still unruffled, pulls his boat smoothly neck and neck with his competitors. Rosemary is feeling a little faint. It almost seems to her that Captain Crummond is *relaxing*, but even so his boat is pulling ahead inch by inch and then yard by yard.

As he passes the winning post the crowd goes wild and Rosemary is weak with admiration, especially when he acknowledges the cheers with an easy, nonchalant wave. He seems to have expended little energy and is sitting up straight-backed as if he has just been for a paddle. In contrast the losers lean or lie crumpled and supine over their oars, like long grass that has been flattened in all directions by a tractor – eight men at the very depths of exhaustion.

Lady Jessica Maltravers gazes at the Henley Hercules with awe. 'He's frightfully dashing!'

'And awfully eligible,' adds Lady Cathleen Hughes-Rotheaton.

'I know,' says Lady Sarah Wartlesby. 'He has simply everything a woman could desire – charm, good lucks and—' she leans forward confidentially, her face a little flushed '… a *very* large legacy.'

Rosemary Fenton sits alone in the opulent palm-filled ballroom of the Phyllis Court Club. Grand arches dominate the bustling tables from which comes the animated chatter of Henley's high society. Waiters in penguin suits flit gracefully from table to table, bowing and scraping to the genteel clientele, while the muted sound of jazz music waft from a small orchestra that plays for the debonair dancers who throng the small dance floor nearby.

Rosemary fidgets with her watch and the locket around her neck, darting nervous glances every few seconds at the doorway. Will he come? Will he notice her? Is everyone noticing her? Is nobody noticing her? Is she invisible? Is this all a dream? What if she should faint at the sight of him? What if he has forgotten she has come to see him?

But then, suddenly, there he is. What a dashing, dapper figure he looks in his natty brown-striped club blazer and cap, white shirt and brown cravat. How the ladies are ogling him, marvelling at his bearing; how all

the men are envying his fine physique. His is the name
on everyone's lips. Stories of his sporting achievements
and legendary exploits are spreading from table to table.
Waiters are vying with one another to catch his eye.

How is he going to notice her? Furtively she waves a
white lace handkerchief to attract his attention, then
glances around guiltily to see if anyone else has seen her.
Nobody has, including Hugh Crummond.

'Do you wish for a table, or are you with a table, sir, or
are you with a party?' the lofty maître d' is asking the
man in the brown-striped blazer in a snooty voice, his
right hand tucked haughtily inside the lapel of his black
jacket with only the white cuff visible. He glances
cursorily at the newcomer and then his face turns red as
he realises whom he is addressing.

'Streuth!' he cries in a broad cockney accent. 'It's
Captain Crummond!'

'I know that face,' says Bullshot, scanning it with his
usual thoroughness.

'Er … Alsop, sir,' replies the maître d' hastily, coming
smartly to attention. 'I was your mechanic in the Flying
Corps, sir,' he adds apologetically. 'You remember the
day you started the propeller while I was still checking
the oil, sir.' With a philosophical grin he points with his
right hand to the white cuff of his left: it is not so much
hidden as absent.

'Sticky moment, sir,' he chuckles. His face – and the
stump at the end of his arm – begin to twitch.

Hugh Crummond can appreciate a good joke. 'Oh, of

course, old boy, ah ha ha ... er, don't bother to salute,'
he adds generously.

Remembering his business, the maître d' asks
deferentially, 'Would you care for a seat by the orchestra,
sir, or out on the terrace?'

'Actually,' confides Bullshot, 'I'm on a case. I'm
joining a Miss Rosemary Fenton.'

'Miss Fenton?' replies the ex-Flying Corps mechanic,
delighted to be of service to his former chief. 'You'll find
'er over there behind the potted palm, sir. Big 'at, spotty
dress.'

'Thank you, Aldwick,' the Captain snaps, falling back
easily into his role of wartime leader.

'—sop,' Alsop corrects him hastily, again falling to
attention.

Crummond looks at him strangely.

'Sir!' remembers the maître d'.

Rosemary is still waving her hankie forlornly, resigned
to an invisible fate, when Hugh Crummond stops at her
table.

'Good afternoon,' he says pleasantly. 'Allow me to
introduce myself. I am—'

She turns to face him. Their eyes meet. Perhaps he
finished introducing himself to her. Perhaps she did the
same. We will never know. The next few seconds are a
blur in which time seems to stand still, sit down and drift
away into some dusty corner of eternity. Somewhere
music plays. Somewhere Henley's idle chitchat witters
on. But here, at this magical table, all is bathed in an

enchanted, iridescent glow. There is no need for words...

To put it bluntly, Captain Hugh 'Bullshot' Crummond, DSO, MC & Bar, late of His Majesty's Royal Loamshires, top ace of the Royal Flying Corps, sports champion and Britain's most decorated hero – and Miss Rosemary Fenton of The Elms, Horsted Keynes, Sussex – have fallen absolutely swimmingly, blissfully, gorgeously, head over heels in love at first sight.

10

In Which Miss Fenton Commits Two Faux Pas and Captain Crummond Passes Two Foes

THE SHEER MAGNITUDE of his overpowering presence took her breath away. Her dreams were all fulfilled – and yet they had been but an overture. With a clash of cymbals, the symphony began. She was ravished, intoxicated, consumed by a master.

It seemed, although she may have imagined it, that Captain Crummond was taking her hand, leaning forward to kiss it. The distance between them closed, their lips were about to touch—

'Menu, sir?'

A menu appeared out of nowhere. Attached to it, the hand of a waiter who slammed it down on the table. The spell was broken, the symphony rudely interrupted.

'Tea and fairy cakes, please, waiter,' Bullshot replied, instantly demonstrating his authority, his presence of mind.

The waiter and Miss Fenton gave him a curious look.

'And a brandy for myself,' he added hastily in a deep voice.

The waiter turned to retrieve the menu that Crummond was holding out at arm's length, anxious for him to be gone. By the time the waiter had hopped behind Hugh's back to seize it, he had impatiently whisked it across to the waiter's original position, forcing the gentleman to do a little dance before unceremoniously clapping his hands over the errant object, as if swatting an irritable fly.

Bullshot returned his attention to Rosemary.

'I gather you're in a spot of bother,' he said solicitously.

Her face fell. She looked away, like a despondent doe.

'Yes, I'm in the most tewwible pwedicament,' she replied softly, her pain evident to Crummond in her desperately feminine sniffles. 'Daddy's been kidnapped…' She began to sob noisily.

Gallantly the Captain checked that he was not being compromised by this little embarrassment. He was: nearby diners were indeed looking.

'Ahhhh!' Rosemary wailed.

'Now, now, Miss Fenton,' he said, anxiously modulating his tone to calm her down and make her be quiet. 'I'm no different from most Englishmen,' he admitted modestly. 'I do so detest a scene in public.'

Rosemary bravely smothered her emotional cataclysm. 'I'm sowwy,' she gasped. 'But they dwove him away in the middle of the night.'

Bullshot raised an eyebrow. 'Did you get a look at the car?'

Rosemary stared into the distance and replied carefully but without hesitation, as if the numbers were engraved on her memory. 'It was a 1928 bwown and black Alvis saloon wegistwation number KT seven, seven, four, thwee.'

Bullshot was impressed. 'That was jolly observant of you, Miss Fenton.'

'It was ours,' she replied with feeling.

He pursed his lips and thought for a moment. 'Of course. It all fits!' he exclaimed. 'And then they transferred him to a Mercedes.'

She marvelled. 'You seem to be one step ahead alweady.'

Bullshot accepted the compliment with good grace. 'When you get to know me better,' he admitted, 'you'll find I usually am.' He patted his cravat. 'But there's one question I have to ask...'

'Yes?' she said expectantly, displaying for his scrutiny the gazelle-like curve of her throat and neck.

'Do you always make a habit of being the most beautiful woman in the room?'

He bowled the compliment with a graceful, underarm motion, following it up by leaning closer towards her.

Rosemary blushed, squirming delicately, and giggled, knocked for six. The man was irresistible.

As this little tête à tête grew warmer, a cold wind seemed to blow into the entrance hall of the Phyllis Court Club ballroom. A tall figure in sham replica of the Club dress, his craggy, monocled visage ferocious and predatory as a wolfhound, accompanied by a painted, slinky female draped in black, approached the maître d'.

'I am looking for Miss Fenton,' hissed Count von Brunno.

The maître d' was the soul of discretion. 'Never 'eard of 'er, sir,' he replied loftily.

Without batting a malevolent eyelid, the Hun advanced a pound note. The maître d' was the soul of discretion.

'You'll find her over there,' he muttered, pocketing the money and turning away. 'Big 'at, spotty dress. Behind the potted palm – with Captain Crummond.'

At the dreaded name, the Black Baron of Blitzburg froze in horror. 'Crummond!' he echoed darkly, and moved quickly aside to observe the couple from behind another potted palm. 'This can mean only one thing. Crummond is on ze case!'

'So!' hissed Lenya, appearing at his shoulder. 'Your

famous adversary is involved in this affair...'

As she peered at the Englishman's athletic form – the black, brilliantined hair, the easy grace and jaunty posture as he sat conversing intimately with the slender, blonde-haired young Englishwoman – the face of the temptress changed colour.

'Ohhhh!' she sighed. 'He is not as you described him.'

The Count eyed her uneasily. 'You find him attractive?'

Like a vulture savouring the scent of her intended prey, she turned slowly to the Count. 'He is *young*,' she breathed.

The Black Baron of Blitzburg scowled and instinctively lifted his hand to his own shiny bald head.

'... So I hid the other half of the formula in this locket,' Rosemary was saying, pointing with her white-gloved hand to the locket, which dangled above her feather-white breast, little knowing that Bullshot was no longer the only recipient of this confidence. Even now the fiendish foreigners were sidling towards their table.

'Then you could be in grave danger, Miss Fenton,' Captain Crummond replied pointedly. 'If my worst suspicions are confirmed, the man behind this is a dastardly Hun called Otto von Brunno.'

The Count slid deceitfully past, his hand shielding his crescent profile from Crummond's gaze.

'And if he knows what you've told me, he could be in the room at this very moment.'

'But would you wecognise him?' Rosemary asked in alarm.

'Not necessarily. It's several years since we last crossed swords. And that was at five thousand feet and he was wearing goggles.'

Rosemary looked anxiously around the ballroom. 'There's no one here with goggles.'

'No, but there are other tell-tale signs that only I would spot,' he reminded her.

'Your brandy, sir,' said the waiter.

It was the one who swatted the menu earlier. A tall,

moustachioed individual with a head like a big loaf of bread, beady, close-set eyes, Gallic nose and round, protruding ears like teapot handles.

'What sort of man is this von Bwunno?'

'Shhhh!' cautioned the Captain, pointing to the waiter. 'He's wearing continental-cut trousers,' he hissed dramatically.

Rosemary stared with consternation at the lower half of the waiter as he returned with her tea. Nonplussed, he served her, giving her an equally suspicious stare. She turns away in fear and embarrassment. The waiter, suddenly aware of her angle of scrutiny, also turned away to check that his fastenings were decent. Risking a second look, she was thrown into further confusion by his digital movements.

'You mean...?' she gasped.

'Too early to say,' Bullshot cautiously replied. 'But his head is just a little too square for my liking.'

'Fairy cakes, sir,' said the waiter wearily, having ascertained that he was correctly buttoned below stairs.

'Thank you. Some soda please,' replied Crummond – and then pointedly, '*Sprechen sie Deutsch?*'

The waiter could not believe his ears. Wheeling round to face Bullshot, he replied in his most superior manner, 'Sir, this is Henley. And at Henley one does *not* speak German,' and walked off disdainfully.

But Hugh Crummond was not a man to be so easily thrown off the scent. 'You see he *knew* it was German I was speaking!' he said victoriously. 'I don't *trust* him. Act naturally.'

He pulled out his pipe and smoked it with marked ostentation, at the same time laughing discreetly, as if at some urbane, sophisticated witticism.

'Ahahahaha!'

Rosemary stared at him blankly.

He laughed again. 'Ahahahahaha!'

Suddenly she cottoned on to the idea and began to cackle, her voice growing progressively louder and higher in pitch.

'Ha ha ha ha ha ha ha!' she pealed piercingly and vibrantly. 'Ha! Ha! Ha! Ha! Ha! Ha! Ha! *Ha!*'

Crummond started to wonder whether the situation might not be getting out of hand, but she was already bound on a wheel of hysteria.

'Ah! Ha! Haw! Ha! Haw! Ha! Haw! Ha! Haw! Ha! Haw! Ha! Haaaah! *Haw! Haw! Haw! Haw! Haw!*'

Diners and dancers were starting to turn. The maître d' looked uncomfortable.

'HA! HA! HA! HA! HEE! ... HA! HA! HA! HA! HEE! ... HA! HA! HA! HA! HA! HEEEEE! *AHAHAHA!*'

Lord Binky Brancaster, dancing the foxtrot with Lady Sarah Wartlesby, turned in wonder. The hyena-like cackles and horsy neighs were coming from his old chum Hugh Crummond's quarters.

'*AW! HAW! HAW! HAW! HAW!*'

'Evidently ze handsome Captain is also humorous,' remarked the Countess dryly.

'No!' the Count snapped. 'This is a diversion to conceal their real intent. We must hear what they are saying.'

'What a beautiful tinkling little laugh you have, Miss Fenton,' Crummond was saying gallantly and with some relief as Rosemary's little gallop into the meadows of hysteria had run its gleeful course and she was finally trotting exhausted back to the tranquil paddocks and restful stables of decent, civilised human intercourse.

But the peace was not to last. The waiter had returned with the soda.

He bent down to siphon it on to Bullshot's brandy. Seizing the moment, Bullshot stood up and blew hard on the hair of the waiter who, teeth clenched, eyes rolling and with all the sang-froid he could muster, perambulated away once more.

'I'm convinced he's wearing a wig!' was Crummond's verdict. 'He may be the master of disguise but he doesn't fool me. Excuse me,' he added as the waiter again passed the table. Leaping up and grabbing his hair, he yanked him down to his knees.

'All right, von Brunno!' he shouted. 'The game's up!'

He tore at the hair once more. In vain. The strain hurt his fingers and he let go, shaking his hand ruefully. With enormous dignity, the waiter pulled himself up to his full height.

'Ouch, sir!' he uttered frostily, patted his hair back into shape, and departed.

'I think your assumptions were wong, Captain,' said Rosemary.

'Not necessarily,' Crummond replied with a shrewd

look in his eyes. 'Oldest trick in the book that, wearing real hair. Now,' he held out his arm and relaxed. 'Let's continue this conversation on the floor.'

'I beg your pardon?' Rosemary was shocked.

'Let's cut a rug,' he explained, a roguish twinkle in his eye.

'Oh, wather!' Rosemary beamed.

They moved to the dance floor and were soon foxtrotting expertly. Though several inches taller than her partner, Rosemary somehow felt safe in the arms of this mesmerising man.

He read her thoughts. 'Much safer here, Miss Fenton, away from eavesdroppers.'

Like two evil birds of prey, the von Brunnos swooped

on to the floor and danced alongside.

'Now, can you recall your father's formula?' Bullshot was immediately down to business.

Rosemary peered at his upturned eyes, only inches below hers, and tried to concentrate. 'Let's think. It started with a capital N and then there was a little A, followed by a teeny little thwee. Then there was a squiggle, a curve, a tick and … I think a hot cwoss bun sign.'

The villainous German vultures greedily digested this, but Hugh Crummond was faster still. 'A sodium dimethyl compound. But with a lower specific gravity!' he exclaimed. Struck by the implications of this he stopped dancing. 'Impossible … and yet…' He resumed dancing.

'I only know it's twemendously important,' said Rosemary helpfully.

'Then you must trust no one. Male *or* female.'

'Why, is there a woman involved?'

'I'm told von Brunno has a wife,' Crummond replied disdainfully. 'At least they went through a *form* of marriage in Bad Gottesburg in 1922.' His nose wrinkled in distaste. 'Heaven knows what kind of unsavoury creature she could be.' He smiled gallantly at the slinky dancer in black who was eyeing him seductively over Rosemary's shoulder.

As the couples swirled around, Rosemary suddenly found herself face to face with the man who had leered through the window of her sitting room. The man who had kidnapped her father. She let out a piercing scream and all at once there was chaos.

'What is it?' cried Bullshot, but she could only point towards the door, whither the evil Count was beating a hasty retreat, bumping into the trolley of the much-abused waiter.

The trolley, bearing an enormous pink cream gateau, wheeled round; the wretched waiter, trying desperately to keep control of it, swung round with it as it collided into the running figure of Captain Crummond, who was nearly knocked off his feet by its momentum.

'You!' Crummond shouted, now firmly convinced that he was facing his long-time foe. 'My God! Scatter everyone! It's a *bomb gateau*!'

Panic and confusion reigned. Even the band gave up trying to play as dancers ran from the floor, knocking over chairs and tables. Bullshot moved back to allow himself maximum run-up and took a flying leap onto the trolley, which, with the pink gateau on board and Bullshot lying flat on both, careered across the floor towards the terrified waiter, who had no chance against such a formidable combination.

The maître d' rushed up to the powerhouse that was Hugh Crummond. 'Thank God you were here, sir,' he shouted. 'You've saved our lives.'

Crummond climbed off the trolley and the gateau, shrugging off both the praise and the pink cream that covered the front of his trousers and blazer.

'Don't mention it, Aldcombe,' he said, looking warily behind the trolley for the waiter, with whom he had unfinished business.

Fortunately for the cowering caterer, who had come within inches of his life, he was spared by Rosemary Fenton, who rushed up to Crummond, waving her arms like a demented windmill.

'Captain Cwummond! *That's* the man who kidnapped Daddy!'

She pointed out of the open door, through which Bullshot could now see two retreating figures.

'*What!*' he bellowed.

Rosemary pointed again. 'The man in the stwiped blazer!' she screamed. But Hugh Crummond had already vanished.

Outside the ballroom he fought his way through a knot of men with striped blazers, all looking suspiciously continental. The nearest moving target happened to be a florid-faced gentleman escorting a young lady: without a moment's hesitation, Crummond brought him crashing to the ground in a magnificent rugby tackle.

'No, sir! That's not 'im, sir! Over there, sir!' called out the dependable Dobbs, never far away in a crisis, through his megaphone, pointing towards the river where Bullshot could see a man and a woman leaping onto the umpire's boat, pushing the umpire into the river as they cast off.

'Loamshire men!' Crummond roared. 'Forward!' He charged down the bank, Dobbs and the maître d' straggling after him and Lord Binky Brancaster bravely bringing up the rear.

But Captain Crummond was once more foiled. With indignant frustration he watched as the boat slipped away down the Thames.

'So it *is* you, von Brunno!' he called out to the Black Baron. 'We meet again!'

With a crooked, malignant grin, the Count lifted his arm in a salute that was calculated to mock and irritate his sworn enemy for years to come.

11

CAPTAIN CRUMMOND pulled up his shiny black Lagonda outside St Ermine's Hotel and jumped out to help Miss Fenton with her suitcases.

'One moment!' he stopped her as she walked through into the lobby. Pretending to be an ordinary person, he seated himself and cast a sharp eye over the clientele.

'All clear,' he reassured her, standing up again.

'Thank you, Captain Crummond. I feel so much safer now,' she sighed, looking down at him with respect and admiration. The events of the day had left her reeling with amazement at the man's ingenuity, daring and savoir faire; was it thus to end? He answered her unspoken question.

'Please – call me Hugh,' he said, looking deeply into her azure eyes. 'And I'll be back for you for you in half an hour … Rosemary.'

Such intimacy of word, look and gesture – indeed the very utterance of her name by such a man as he – made her palpitate with pleasure in odd little nooks and crannies of her being. She stopped him as he made to leave: she had to let him know.

'You're so tewibly bwave,' she said. 'Nothing seems to fwighten you.'

'Hmmmm?' he asked, puzzled.

'Fwighten you,' she repeated.

'Sorry, old girl,' Bullshot replied, gazing stoically into the far distance where even now dark forces lurked, threatening the very fabric of civilisation, and wondering whether the gal could perhaps benefit from a few elocution lessons. 'Don't know the meaning of the word.'

He gave her arm a reassuring squeeze and departed, leaving Miss Fenton teetering on the borderline between ecstasy and bliss.

'Where is this case taking us, sir?' asked Dobbs, emerging from his master's dressing room, carrying a number of Captain Crummond's finest checked suits on hangers.

Bullshot finished cleaning and servicing his Webley pistol. He had never left anything to chance, ever since the Mongolian mangler had trounced him in the Urals.

'We're picking up Miss Fenton at her hotel —'

'Perhaps the Prince of Wales check for that, sir,' suggested the gentleman's gentleman.

'Then we're off to her home in Sussex,' the Captain continued, sticking something big inside the barrel.

'Sussex...' Dobbs pondered. 'The Birdseye or the Hound's tooth...'

'Later we may have a quiet dinner,' Crummond added casually, pulling it out and blowing.

'Dinner jacket and black tie, sir,' Dobbs called from the dressing room.

As Bullshot was giving his pistol a final rub, the doorbell rang.

'Is Captain Crummond in?' he heard the visitor enquire.

He frowned, packed the Webley into his pocket and moved nearer to the door to listen.

'Who shall I say is calling, sir?' asked Dobbs.

A man in a long overcoat, bowler hat, spectacles and moustache entered the living room. Crummond swung round to face him.

'Scotland Yard,' said the visitor gruffly.

'Come this way, sir.

'Good afternoon, Captain Crummond. I'm Jeffcock of ze Yard,' said the visitor, holding out his hand.

Bullshot attempted to shake it but the visitor merely flashed an identity card, quickly whisking it back into his overcoat pocket before the Captain could inspect it.

'Colonel Hinchcliff sent me.'

'Sir Robert, really?' Bullshot replied, relaxing. 'Drink?' he asked genially.

'Zank you.'

'Scotch?'

'Splendid,' said the visitor, removing his bowler and the hair attached to it, which Dobbs dutifully took to hang on the hat stand in the hall, leaving Count Otto von Brunno's shiny baldness exposed for Crummond's perusal.

'Ice?' asked Bullshot, busy pouring drinks at the sideboard.

'Never,' von Brunno replied resolutely.

'So what brings Scotland Yard to this neck of the Kensington woods?' Crummond asked good-humouredly.

'Oh, it's ze Fenton case.'

'What about it?'

'It's a highly sensitive matter.' The Count walked over to Bullshot, who still had his back to him. 'We want you to stay out of it.'

He glanced in the mirror above the sideboard, caught sight of his own bald head, ducked in horror and darted back to the hall to retrieve his wig.

'I'm sorry,' Crummond was saying. 'I can't do that. I gave my word to a lady – and what an impeccably pedigreed little filly she is.' He turned to present the Count with his scotch.

'I'm afraid I must ask you to keep your personal feelings out of this,' snapped the re-wigged Count. 'The safety of *England* is at stake.'

The word may have been pronounced rather oddly but it had a mystical effect on Hugh Crummond. He stiffened, raised himself to his full height – as if about to sing the National Anthem.

'England!' he echoed, and walked over to gaze at the memorabilia over his mantelpiece, a homage to all that he held dear, and once again turned his back on the dissembling Hun, who quickly patted his wig in place before the mirror. 'That puts a very different complexion on things...' He deliberated as the Black Baron quickly touched up his cheeks with theatrical paint.

Bullshot suddenly seemed to come to a decision.

'Very well, you leave me no choice,' he said grimly.

An evil grin swept over the Count's face. He wiped it off a second later as Crummond swung round again – a changed man.

'Your country will never forget you, Captain,' he predicted – for once without deceit. 'Just for ze record, old chap—' he assumed a careless tone '—did Miss Fenton tell you anything?'

'Not much,' Bullshot admitted – for once without false modesty. 'Except that she had half her father's formula hidden in the locket around her neck.'

'Haaaa!' the Count exploded exultantly, clenching his fist, and quickly disguising his triumph in a fit of coughing. 'I hope we can rely on you, Captain,' he added after a suitable interval.

Crummond was shocked. 'Inspector Jeffcock, I think you will find that I am not a man to go back on my word.'

12

In Which the Cunning Arm of Blind Fate Starts a Taxi and Stops a Bus

'CAPTAIN CRUMMOND, how could you go back on your word?' protested Rosemary tearfully, slamming her teacup down on the tearoom table of the St Ermine's Hotel. Dressed in sensible tweed hat and coat, she had been preparing to return to Horsted Keynes, trusting in the Captain to do what was necessary. *The one man in England we can trust*, Daddy had said.

But it seemed she had been wrong. Hugh Crummond, it now turned out, had more important things to do. And he had just made that clear to her in so many words. Now there was no one she could trust. It was all too awful.

Bullshot could not bear to look at her, dreading that at any moment she would break out into those terrible sobs again. Henley had been bad enough. He stood stiffly to attention, as if being court-martialled for a crime he had not committed.

'Nothing has ever disturbed me more, Miss Fenton,' he vowed.

'I at least have the wight to know why you're now not going to help me.'

He swallowed: as one who liked to play the ball straight down the middle it hurt to have to lie to a chap on his own side, but this was a matter of national security – and his own reputation.

'I promised my chum we'd enter the London to Brighton rally.' It was a half-truth. 'It was a prior commitment.' He glanced quickly at her: her stumps were down, but only just.

'How can you stand there and talk about *gweasy* motor cars when *Daddy's in pewil!*'

He had to admit it: the gal had pluck. And, dammit, she was right. How could he make her understand without giving the show away? He tried again. 'Believe me I—'

'I thought you were a hewo,' Rosemary cut through him, picking up her red cape and making for the door. 'I can see now I was wrong. You're nothing more than an overgwown schoolboy who would wather play with his marbles than help a woman who has fallen deeply in – *oh!*'

Mortified by this virtual admission of her true feelings, Rosemary burst into tears and dashed out of the door, down the stairs and into the sedate hotel lobby where Hugh caught up with her.

Rosemary's visions of the Captain as a knight in shining armour riding on his white charger to the rescue of her father were gone for a Burton, while she herself had, as it were, been trampled underfoot. But if Lancelot couldn't, Guinevere could.

'I never thought I'd see the day when a woman would have to stand up for herself,' she sobbed. 'I see I'll have to wescue Daddy without you.' She gave another little sniff and headed out of the hotel door.

'Taxi!' she called out, and one drew up immediately.

Overcome with the passion and the absurdity of her last speech, Bullshot chased after her.

'Rosemary, wait, I'll come clean … it's—' he blurted out impulsively as the doorman loaded her baggage into the taxi.

She turned expectantly, her face lit up. 'Yes?'

'It's…'

Dash it, he thought, *how can I let the side down now?*

'*Yes*?' cried Rosemary, her face flushed and excited.

But Captain Crummond was spared the agony of compromising himself and his country by the strains of a patriotic march from across the street. Abandoning Rosemary to her suspense he turned to look.

Along the road came a band of ex-servicemen buskers – a motley crew of five or six one-armed, one-legged, blind, deaf or dumb war-wounded veterans in threadbare uniforms bedecked with medals. One played a concertina, another the trumpet; a third, wearing a red fez and striped nightgown, was floppily performing the Egyptian sand dance; another carried a sorry-looking flag and yet another a big bass drum bearing the words 'Royal Loamshire Regiment' and the Latin inscription '*In Pace Semper Tedium Est*'.

Captain Crummond could hardly contain himself. Here they all were again, all the chaps who mattered, the bravest and the finest – give or take a limb or two and a couple of gallant chaps who'd gone before. With a tear of pride he sprang to attention.

'Look!' he yelled excitedly to Rosemary. 'There's some chaps from my old regiment, the Royal Loamshires. Look—' he pointed '—there's Cunningham and Erskine ... and Dusty Miller.'

'Did I ever tell you about the time I did a daisy-cutter in the old Camel?' he reminisced nostalgically, turning back to Rosemary – but Miss Fenton had at last abandoned all hope and was already speeding away in the taxi.

Torn between love and duty, Crummond sighed wretchedly. But the buskers had stopped playing and Erskine had recognised the man they used to hero worship in the trenches.

'Look!' he exclaimed. 'There's Captain Crummond! If it wasn't for him, we wouldn't be where we are today.'

The buskers snapped paraplegically to attention, each in their own way cherishing their memories and each, as best they could, saluting their former leader.

Cunningham, whose vision was obscured by the bass drum strapped round his chest, held out his one remaining arm. 'Captain Crummond,' he called out hoarsely, 'is it really you? Let me shake you by the hand, sir.'

For a moment Cunningham hesitated to cross the road as he listened for traffic. But Bullshot, filled with warmth and bonhomie, would have none of it.

'Don't worry, laddie,' he called back cheerily, 'there's no land mines in Mayfair!'

Cautiously Cunningham started to cross the road,

moving awkwardly behind the drum, which, sadly, had no eyes to see the omnibus that appeared out of nowhere. With a squeal of brakes it mowed the unfortunate veteran down in his moment of glory – separating him forever from his bass drum, which rolled remorselessly across the road towards Crummond, knocking the Captain over onto the pavement.

Hastily clambering to his feet, Bullshot scowled at the drum and at the perpetrators of this embarrassment: it just would not do to be caught with one's trousers down in front of the chaps. Bad for the morale.

In a superbly smooth-flowing follow-through gesture, he retrieved three-quarters of his dignity by performing a loose half-bend, giving him the opportunity to straighten his jacket, smooth his trousers, and appear ready for the next obstacle. Pulling himself up to his full height, he ostentatiously snatched at his cuff to glare at his watch, and marched off, head in the air.

The dazzling display was lost on the ex-servicemen, who stood in stunned disbelief, hands covering the eyes of those who had not lost them in the trenches.

Only now could they begin to appreciate just how much, in his heroic and never-ending struggle to defend their beloved British Empire from those who sought to undermine it, Bullshot Crummond was prepared, without counting the cost, to sacrifice himself – and with what courage and fortitude he had faced the bitter task of teaching them just how much in return he would demand of those who would follow in his wake, even down to the ultimate sacrifice of the most humble of their kind.

'Dobbs! Where are you?' thundered Hugh Crummond, angrily flinging open the door to his Mayfair chambers and striding through to the living room. 'I need a drink. It's been a *hellish* day.'

Though surprised in a state of undress, the shirtsleeved, waistcoated vassal stood waiting miraculously with a glass of scotch on a silver tray in his palm to greet his master's unexpected arrival.

'I'm afraid it's not over yet, guv'nor,' he replied evenly.

'What!' Bullshot exploded.

'I found these in the rubbish downstairs,' said the valet, revealing in his other hand the Count's hat and wig. 'Recognise 'em?'

'Heavens!' cried Crummond, sniffing them like a hound unleashed. 'The chap from Scotland Yard!'

'Colonel Hinchcliff never sent him, sir. Look.' He handed his master a copy of *The Times*.

Bullshot looked disgusted. 'That's the last straw,' he said in despair. '"England crushed by Australia".'

'No sir, not the cricket. Above that. "Red faces at
Yard. Sir Robert Hinchcliff found with knife in back.
Foul play suspected",' he quoted verbatim.

'My God!' roared Hugh Crummond. 'Rosemary!'

13

IN WHICH LENYA VON BRUNNO IS CAUGHT IN HER BAD HABITS AND THE BLACK BARON OF BLITZBURG EXPOSES HIMSELF

M ISS ROSEMARY FENTON sat alone by the window in a first-class compartment as the Sussex-bound train hurtled through the English countryside.

Try as she might, she was unable to erase the memory of Captain Crummond as he stood before her outside the hotel – hands on hips, short but powerful legs astride, chest pushed forward as he surveyed with curious pride the disreputable band of oafs staggering along the road. Her feelings overwhelmed her. It was as though she were wrestling with some elementary force of nature and she was a mere human being – and a woman at that.

Who were these people and what did they have to do with Daddy? How could he abandon her for a silly car ride? Had she been unfair? She thought not, but – what was it he was going to come clean about? Was there something she didn't know?

She sighed: there were so many things she didn't know about Captain Hugh Crummond and she was not likely to find out now. From the moment she had stepped into the taxi she had known that from now on it was all up to her. She had sworn to rescue Daddy – but how?

The carriage door slid open with a sinister, grating sound and Rosemary looked up apprehensively. To her relief she saw that her fellow passengers were priests – or to be more precise, a priest and a nun. They smiled with ingratiating benevolence, the black robed priest taking the window seat opposite her. The nun, a strikingly tall and curiously attractive sister of mercy, draped her voluminous habit by the seat next to the door, crossing her slender legs and depositing her umbrella beside her.

To her surprise – and then to her mounting horror – Rosemary's eyes and those of nun met. There was no mistaking the carefully applied mascara, the rouged cheeks, nor the scarlet lipstick. And were not those eyebrows *plucked*?

Trust no one. Male or female. Hugh's warning echoed through her mind as, with beating heart, she now perceived the long, varnished fingernails and finally, horror of horrors, the seductive and unwholesomely decadent stiletto heels and rhinestone-studded anklets binding the black stockings.

'Vot a charming locket, my dear,' the priest opposite her suddenly said, in an accent that might have been Irish, but had a hint of something else – a suspicious trace of the continental. 'Is it a Saint Christopher?'

He leaned forward with a jerk to finger her precious treasure *and then she recognised him.*

Jumping to her feet, she let out a piercing scream as the contorted, diabolical features of Count Otto von Brunno leered up at her.

'Get away from me!' she gasped as she backed away from the carriage windows, with great presence of mind grabbing Lenya von Brunno's umbrella to defend herself.

But his wicked accomplice was already pulling down the blinds as the Black Baron of Blitzburg lunged for the locket and broke the chain. 'Quick, Lenya!' he barked. 'I have ze locket, now throw her out!'

Desperately she fought with the Count as Lenya opened the carriage door. With surprising tenacity the Englishwoman bit the Black Baron's earlobe, making him howl with rage; with astonishing agility she kicked the Countess, who was seizing her from behind, in the calf; with courageous defiance Rosemary spat at them, but finally the brute strength and deceitful guile of the Hun were too much for her.

With an evil roar of triumph that was lost in the noise of the thundering train, the fiendish Germans pushed Miss Fenton backwards through the open carriage door to a certain death…

14

IN WHICH THE HUN ARE SCOTCHED BY A ROEDEAN DONWPOUR AND A SCOTSMAN IS POURED DOWN UNDER THE ROAD

B
UT THE PHILISTINES had reckoned without the finest boarding school for well-bred young ladies in the civilised world. If the Lawrence sisters of Roedean School, Brighton, had taught Rosemary Fenton one lesson, it was the art of opening up an umbrella in the nick of time to avoid the sudden, fickle inclemencies of cloudbursts during croquet matches.

Just before Rosemary was ejected onto the rails, she hastily levered the mechanism: the canopy mushroomed open inside the carriage before the startled eyes of the Hun. Too large and stiff to fit through the door, it anchored her to the train as she fell backwards, still clinging to the umbrella handle. With her feet still resting on the carriage door, the trusty tool supported her weight as she leaned outwards at an angle of forty-five degrees.

With a piercing screech of its whistle the train entered a tunnel. In the hellish blackness the conspiring Krauts used every ounce of their strength in a vain attempt to push the umbrella out of the door, but they had not taken into account the British workmanship that had gone into its manufacture. Not for nothing was the co-operation between the common British working man, the scientists and engineers and the organisational skills of the superior classes who employed his labour the envy of the world in comparison with the inferior, shoddy product of the continental mind.

The Treadaway and Harbottle umbrella was a labour of love, as sturdy as Nelson's Column. Proud to be British, it stuck to its task of bolstering up Miss Fenton against the brutish Hun.

But Rosemary was fast losing the battle. In the infernal darkness and smoke of the tunnel, she was swept to one side. Still clinging with one hand to the dependable handle, she resourcefully grabbed the rain gutter above her with the other. At that moment, by a quirk of fate, the Count at last managed to kick the umbrella through the door, little knowing that he was too late.

The umbrella handle, finally broken by its exertions against the mindless muscle of the Hun, had fought the good fight and given of its best. Knowing that it had played its small but important part, like a humble private, it was proud to die an unsung hero: its neck snapped, but the corpse of its handle stuck doggedly, loyally and faithfully by Rosemary, even as her one-handed grasp of the rain gutter was weakening.

Inside the compartment, the Count and Lenya laughed with malevolent gratification.

'Hurry, Lenya, close ze door!' roared von Brunno.

They pulled on the leather strap and the door was shut.

'Good! She is gone!' he growled. 'And I have ze locket!' He held it up in triumph.

'Poor little English rose,' sneered Lenya. 'She was so *beautiful*. Captain Crummond will be heartbroken.'

The Count lifted down Rosemary's suitcases from the luggage rack. 'Doubtless he will claim her things,' he smirked. 'Imagine his face when he discovers our little surprise…'

They chuckled hideously.

'Good practice for the London to Brighton, sir,' shouted Dobbs above the engine roar of Captain Crummond's black Lagonda. He studied the map while Crummond, in brown leather RFC coat, scarf sticking out stiffly behind him in the breeze, pipe sticking out stiffly in his mouth, steered the open tourer expertly along the English country road.

'If you keep this speed up we'll get to Horsted Keynes only two minutes after Miss Fenton's train.'

Bullshot's eyes were fixed on the distant skyline.

'That may be two minutes too late, Dobbs,' he shouted back grimly. 'I'll wager a halfpenny bun to a pound of dried bananas that Miss Fenton is in deadly peril!'

Still clinging tenaciously to the rain gutter, Rosemary painfully edged her way, inches at a time, towards the next compartment. When she finally reached it, her hands aching as though they had been run over by a horse, she peered through the slightly open window, transferring one hand to the top of the glass.

To her joy she saw that there was someone inside. She tapped urgently on the window with the umbrella handle but, to her dismay, the occupant didn't react. Again she rapped and at last the figure stirred and stood up. He was a towering giant of a man, who picked up a white cane and started fumbling for the door handle. Evidently he was blind.

'Horsted Keynes? Already?' he grumbled in a loud, gruff Scottish accent: he was a man-mountain in kilt and beret with a full-blooded bearing, thick, overgrown Iago-style moustache and beard and rugged northern features. He finally managed to open the door, swinging the petrified, hysterical Miss Fenton away from the carriage.

'Thank you, Porter,' he called out cheerily. 'Windy tonight, isn't it. Come along, Hamish.'

In a corner of the carriage his Scottish terrier, wrapped in a tiny tartan blanket, whimpered a warning.

'What's the matter with ye?' cried the fearless, eyeless Highlander.

'Help!' Rosemary screamed desperately.

'No thank you,' he replied with amiable stoicism, stepping loftily out of the train and disappearing with a loud scream as the train hurtled on.

Hamish stood at the open door, watching his blind master departing from his sight for ever, then lay down on the seat, covering his eyes with his paws.

Outside the compartment Rosemary was wedged between the train and the open carriage door, whose windows she now clung to with gritty English tenacity and blistered fingers.

The blind man tumbled down the soft, grassy embankment, landing with a thud on the country road below. Picking himself up, he just had time to dust himself down when a motor car bore down on him, bleeping its horn impatiently. Scrambling out of the way, the Scotsman performed a little jig in the middle of the road before tumbling in a somersault into the ditch on the other side.

Hugh Crummond's Lagonda, which had been running neck and neck with the train and was about to overtake it, swerved wildly through an enormous puddle, sending a shower of muddy water cascading over the hapless Highlander. The open tourer screeched to a halt.

'What the devil do you think you're doing?' Bullshot demanded. 'You could have had us all killed!'

The blind man stood up, cocking his head in the air. 'I know that voice,' he said excitedly. 'It's the Captain! It's Captain Crummond!' He strode towards the car, tapping the road viciously with his white stick.

'What if it is?' Crummond replied impatiently.

'It's me, sir,' said the Scot, waving his white stick around horizontally, obliging the Captain and his manservant to duck, dodge and weave their heads to avoid having them bashed to bits by the eyeless warrior. 'McGilliecuddy, sir!'

'Surely not *Hawkeye* McGilliecuddy?' Bullshot said in wonder.

'Used to be, sir,' Hawkeye replied with cheerful nostalgia, 'until ye sent me doon that rabbit hole, to see if there was live ammunition in it. They gave me a medal for it, sir,' he added proudly, arms by his side, sightless eyes raised to the sky.

Crummond tapped the dashboard impatiently.

'Memory Lane will have to keep for another day, Hawkeye,' he declared briskly but not unkindly as he remembered how the man's telescopic vision had struck fear and dread in the hearts of every Hun a hundred miles around. 'Jump aboard and hold on tight.'

He revved up the engine and drove off, leaving Hawkeye to dive as best he could head-first into the back seat.

15

In Which Hawkeye McGilliecuddy Falls into a Tree, Captain Crummond falls into a Window and Miss Rosemary Fenton Falls into a Swoon

'HORSTED KEYNES!' called the guard.

The train chugged and chuffed to a halt. Still in their priestly robes, the two Germans slunk out of the carriage, skulked down the platform and sidled through the barrier, swallowed up by the crowd.

The guard walked alongside the train, closing the doors behind departing passengers. When he came to the last one, he swung it back to discover Rosemary Fenton attached to it. He regarded her blandly.

'Well, what do you know?' he said in his slow, weary country accent. 'Don't you know it's against railway regulations to open the door before the train stops?'

She could hardly speak from exhaustion.

'I'm awfully sowwy, I … er … could you help me down, please?'

'Very well,' he said, lowering her to the platform like a bothersome piece of lost luggage. Still glued to the stump of umbrella handle, she stood like a statue with both arms fixed rigidly above her head.

'I hope you've learnt your lesson,' he said kindly, pulling them down in mild reproof.

'Did you see that?' Bullshot enquired of his passengers as they careered down a side road that led to Horsted Keynes.

'No,' replied the blind man with absolute confidence and complete certainty.

'A taxi with no passengers heading in a westerly direction, driven by a man with no ears...' He raised his eyebrow. 'Of course!'

'Left at the crossroads for "The Elms", sir,' inserted Dobbs.

'Miss Fenton won't be there, Dobbs, because today is Thursday,' Crummond replied, looking rather pleased with himself.

'What's Thursday got to do with it, guv?'

'Remember Corporal Billington, back in the Loamshires?'

'The chap who lost his ears in the Western Front?' said Dobbs.

'Yes, Dougie Billington.'

'We used to call him Lugless Douglas,' the ex-private reminisced.

'I often bump into him,' called out Hawkeye from the back of the car, his dark glasses twinkling in the late afternoon sunshine. 'I can't see him and he can't hear me coming.'

'I happen to know that he runs the only taxi in the village,' Bullshot went on. 'And every Thursday he plays billiards at Cuckfield.' He was pulling up outside an old picturesque country inn with white walls and ivy-covered bay windows. 'So Rosemary would have to stay here, at the Whippet Inn,' he concluded triumphantly, climbing out of the Lagonda, followed by Dobbs.

'Come along, Hawkeye,' the Captain called out after him, for the blind Scotsman was happily wandering off in the wrong direction, away from the inn, whipping his white stick wildly through the air and nearly knocking a passing cyclist off his bike.

Crummond led the way through to the rear garden, where bees droned lazily around the rose bushes in the golden sunset.

'She would have picked Room 36,' he announced.

'How d'you work that out, guv'nor?' asked Dobbs.

'She'll be needing an early start tomorrow so she would have picked an easterly room that gets the morning sun…'

Dobbs followed the direction of his arm, while Hawkeye turned and peered in the opposite direction.

An elderly woman with a pinched, anxious face looked out of the window and, seeing Captain Crummond pointing at her, drew the curtains in hasty alarm.

'I think your calculations were a bit off, Captain,' said Dobbs with a guilty grin.

'Not at all, Dobbs,' Bullshot replied, unperturbed. 'I said "*would* have picked Room 36". However, if she suspected von Brunno was following her, she would have changed her plans and chosen Room 27.' He pointed in another direction. 'There!'

As by some prearranged signal, Rosemary Fenton appeared at the open window of Room 27 and leaned out to close it. Crummond nodded his head jauntily at Dobbs.

Hawkeye had been following his own eccentric course round the garden, his cane describing wide arcs to clear the path for his bizarre zigzagging meanderings.

'Can I help, sir?' he asked cheerfully. 'It'd be just like old times.'

'Good show, Hawkeye!' Bullshot boomed genially. 'I'll rescue Rosemary. You keep lookout.'

'Yes, *sir*,' responded the obedient Highlander, stamping his feet to attention and shouldering his white stick like a guard with a rifle on sentry duty. Wheeling sharply, he marched off with devastating military precision, disappearing into the thick, embracing foliage of a fir tree and was never seen again.

Crummond, using Dobbs's back as a stepping stone, hauled himself up athletically to the rose trellis above the bay window of the dining room, which was beneath Rosemary's window.

Suddenly, he lost his balance and for a moment elderly guests eating their evening meals were afforded a view of a pair of legs hanging upside down at the window. The legs quickly vanished from sight, but those of a more nervous disposition had to be helped to their beds.

Inside her room Rosemary Fenton was about to open the twin locks of her suitcases and of her life. She was vibrant, she was alone, she was free. She could climb mountains or become prime minister. She would achieve immortal fame, accomplish legendary feats. The world would be her oyster: she would fly round it and conquer it like Amy Johnson. There would be no more dark clouds in her sky, no conceited men barging their way on to her horizon.

Inspired, she turned to the window to see the beaming face of Hugh Crummond, his arms waving like windmills.

'Captain Cwummond!' she called out in astonishment and horror. 'What on earth are you doing here?'

'I'm back on the case, Rosemary,' he replied with a modest grin.

'Thank you, but your services are no longer wequired,' Rosemary dismissed him frostily and closed the window.

Flabbergasted, Bullshot quickly turned to check that he had not been observed in this humiliating position. A number of guests had gathered in the back garden, curious to find out what was happening and pointing up at him. He tapped hastily on the window again until Miss Fenton finally relented.

'I see,' he said immediately. 'So you're going to do battle with the most dangerous man in the world, single-handed.'

'And why not?' she enquired haughtily, crossing her arms.

Hugh Crummond's patience was stretched to the limit.

'Have you even given a moment's thought to what you're going to use for *brains*?'

Rosemary was livid. 'How *dare* you!' she shouted. 'I'll have you know I've been doing *pwetty* well without bwains so far, independent of male supports. Who needs men? Times are changing, Hugh Cwummond. I feel it in my *bweast*.'

Crummond flinched. 'Rosemary! Please!' he cautioned. 'That's trench language!'

'Yes, Hugh, *bweast*!' She shrieked the word with piercing clarity. 'Not the soft words of the housewife or the flapper, but the twue, exposed words of a new woman.' She lifted her hands to her quivering bosom to emphasise her passionate points, and added, 'A *naked* woman!'

Abashed, aghast, Bullshot turned to the hotel guests below.

'No need for alarm!' he assured them. 'I'm a collector of unusual insects!'

But Miss Fenton was in full flight. 'A woman of the future,' she declaimed romantically. 'A lone figure in Oxford bags and no *bwassiere*.'

The crowd below was growing larger.

'A rare breed of moths!' he called out hastily.

Rosemary was not to be silenced. '... Soon to be joined in her march to fweedom by her sisters, who will eat and sleep together and dwive twactors for a living. I hope to be one of those women.' She glanced disdainfully down at Crummond. 'Who needs a man's *cwutch*? Your sex is all washed up. This is my show now!'

Hugh chuckled for the benefit of the large crowd who were now quite stirred by Rosemary's impassioned speech.

'Carry on about your business, ha, ha, ha, ha, ha!' he chortled desperately, turning to face them. By the time he had turned back to the window, Rosemary had again slammed it shut.

Seconds later a piercing scream came from the room.

'What is it, Rosemary?' he called out, at last managing to open the window. But in doing so, he lost his balance and began to fall through the trellis.

'Oh, isn't that romantic?' said one elderly lady to another. 'Just like Romeo and Juliet.'

Hugh Crummond was not a man to cave in under stress. He sprang back to the ledge and dived head-first into the room. Rosemary was standing by the bed, holding up her hands in horror.

'*Something... something moved inside my suitcase!*' she screamed.

Bullshot took a close look: the lid was indeed bouncing up and down. He immediately took charge.

'Stand back, Rosemary, it could be alive!' he warned her, interposing himself between the Englishwoman and her baggage before bravely throwing open the lid.

He jumped back in alarm. 'Good God!' he gasped. 'Is there no end to the fiendish jiggery-pokery of these von Brunnos?'

'What *is* it?' Rosemary squeaked, her hands covering her eyes, her back turned to the as-yet unnamed horror.

Hugh Crummond turned to the quaking female and took a deep breath. 'Brace yourself, Rosemary. It's an *arachnid hirsutis* – the deadly tarantula!'

At that moment the huge, hairy little beast, which had been nestling on top of Rosemary's clothing, scurried to the edge of the suitcase and leapt out on to the floor.

As though the Black Baron were here in the room, the atrocious object, with a malice that was more intelligent than any insect, more deadly than any human, flickered its foul fangs and started to crawl venomously towards Hugh Crummond and Rosemary Fenton – on a journey that could end only in madness – *or in death.*

16

'OH, IT'S A TAWANTULA,' sighed Rosemary, smiling fondly and walking round the bed to cuddle it. 'Daddy used to expewiment with them. You can easily pawalyse them by thwowing talcum powder on their backs.'

She put out her hand to stroke it but Hugh Crummond was a human barricade. 'Stand clear, Rosemary!' he bellowed. Driving tractors is one thing. This is *man's* work!'

Like lightning he whisked out his Webley and fired several shots at the floor where the tarantula was lurking, blowing large holes through into the ceiling of the dining room below. The hotel guests, mostly well past retirement age, blanched in horror as chunks of wood, plaster and distemper fell from the ceiling into their chicken soup, smashing plates and spilling hot liquid over their clothes and skin.

The ear-shattering sound of gunshot was to disturb for the few years left to them their rock-solid faith in the sombre ritual of dinner. A white-jacketed waiter ran in circles like a frightened car. A red-faced ex-army colonel hid under a table, much to the alarm of two elderly ladies who screamed in fright. Guests jumped up in horror and then stood petrified, their hands covering their ears. Others tried to calm them down, and then had hysterics themselves.

'Strike a light, streuth, cor blimey!' shouted Dobbs as he burst into the room. 'What's goin' on 'ere?'

'Some maniac is shooting at us,' replied the manageress, Miss Roberts, a refined lady with piercing blue eyes and strings of pearls.

'You're in luck, lady, 'cos Captain "Bullshot" Crummond is on the premises.'

A great cheer arose from the previously terrified guests and a buzz of excitement spread around the hotel. Little cries of 'bravo' could still be heard as Miss Roberts, herself greatly relieved, sought to instil some order to the proceedings.

'Calm down, everybody,' she called out in a slow, dignified and patronising voice, as though addressing a class of unruly eight-year-olds. But a blush of expectation was spreading over her porcelain cheeks.

Followed by the chef, the waiter and the manageress, Dobbs raced from room to room, dodging another hail of bullets, in search of Captain Crummond, their only hope.

'There you are, Rosemary,' Bullshot announced after firing one last shot at the spider. 'He's done for.' He bent down to examine its bullet-ridden carcase, satisfied with his handiwork.

'Be careful, Hugh!' she warned. 'Tawantulas often play dead. Here's the talcum.'

Captain Crummond brushed the tin aside and picked up the immobile spider. 'No need for that,' he said suavely. 'Look, dead as a doornail! ... AAArrrgghh!' he yelled as the spiteful little beast bit him.

Still clutching and clutched by the spider, he threatened it with his pistol, bravely unconcerned by the possibility that he might blast off his own hand.

'No, Hugh!' screamed Rosemary, unable to stand idly by and watch him make such a sacrifice. She swung his arm aside just as the door was flung open by Dobbs. Outside in the corridor the manageress, the chef, the waiter and the two elderly ladies clung together as Crummond again fired his Webley. A wall sconce behind him shattered into little pieces.

'My word!' said Miss Roberts, rushing into the room, thrilled at this chance of a lifetime. 'It is the brave Captain Crummond in person.'

'At your service, madam,' Bullshot replied nonchalantly.

'We need your help,' she declared in her slow, careful, stately way, as though she were Queen Victoria summoning Disraeli to the defence of the Empire. Rosemary thought she'd make a simply spiffing headmistress.

'There's a maniac loose in the hotel,' Miss Roberts explained confidentially. 'And he has a gun!'

'What!' Crummond exploded. Was it possible? Could the Hun really stoop so low in his criminal quest as to butcher in cold blood these defenceless old folk in the Indian summer of their lives? The man was a monster who had to be stopped.

His blood was up and with the instincts of a trained killer he waved his Webley above his head. Rosemary quickly spilled talc on the spider, which fell from his hand dead on the floor. She stamped on it.

Captain Crummond raced across the landing to the staircase but his progress was impeded by a crowd of hotel staff and guests. Undaunted, the Captain leapt on to the banister rail and slid down it with the agility of an experienced mountaineer, crashing into the huge, round newel post at the foot of the stairs.

The damage to the lower portion of his anatomy would have put an end to the matrimonial pleasures of a lesser man, but Bullshot was made of harder stuff. Even so, as he dismounted and sunk to his knees, face ashen with shock, he was unable to answer Miss Roberts's solicitous 'Captain Crummond, were you shot?', but could only bravely nod as he staggered to his knees.

The dining room was a shambles. Tables were overturned with half-eaten plates of dinner strewn about the polished floor. Bullet holes studded the walls, floor and ceiling, and several window panes were broken. Still dazed from his encounter with the newel post, Crummond led the way, followed in a conga line by Rosemary, Dobbs, Miss Roberts, the chef, the waiter, the porter, the cleaning lady, several guests, a chauffeur and the commissionaire.

'Is it safe?' whispered the colonel, his head emerging from under a tablecloth.

'Oh, it's all right, Colonel,' the manageress reassured him calmly. 'You can come out now.'

'Look!' Rosemary exclaimed, pointing to a circle of bullet holes in the centre of the ceiling, which had brought the chandelier crashing down to the floor. Bullshot rushed over to inspect this piece of vandalism.

'Von Brunno's nasty work!' he said indignantly. 'It's one thing trying to kill *me*; but to endanger the lives of innocent people ... despicable!'

He climbed onto a chair and all at once was a human theodolite, a wizard of navigation as he aimed and angled his arms and legs like rulers and compasses. The assembly looked on in awe.

'What are you doing, Hugh?' asked Rosemary in astonishment.

'I took the precaution of studying the blueprints of every hotel between here and London—' the pistol was pointing lethally in all directions as he continued the strange configurations '—and judging from the trajectory of the bullets, they were fired from Room 27.'

'But that's my room...' Rosemary replied doubtfully.

'What!' thundered the Captain, jumping off the chair and charging for the door. 'There's no time to be lost.

Von Brunno may be there. Hurry!'

The conga line of staff and guests, growing longer all the time, followed like a wriggling appendage as he leaped up the stairs and tiptoed nimbly along the landing. Stopping outside Rosemary's door, he stepped back dramatically. The conga line behind him shuffled backwards, those on the stairs landing like a pack of cards in a heap on the entry hall floor.

'Stay back!' he whispered tensely. 'Von Brunno's probably hiding.'

With the stealth of a tiger he entered the room and silently moved about it. Suddenly he pounced on the single bed and upended it, sending it crashing through the window.

'All right, von Brunno!' he announced theatrically. 'The show's over!' He fired the gun at the ceiling: a crescendo of nervous screams concertinaed along the landing and down the stairs as the ceiling lamp exploded and shattered in all directions. Leaping at the curtains, he tore them down in one movement. There was nothing behind them. He paused and raised an eyebrow.

Clambering stealthily to the wardrobe, he tripped over the upended bed and reached out wildly to grasp the white-enamelled bedroom washbasin to keep his balance, tearing it from its hinges. Water gushed from the broken pipes.

By now the staff and guests were hysterical, but Captain Crummond had nerves of steel. And he wasn't finished yet.

'I know you're in there!' he threatened the wardrobe, grasping the top, which, after a reluctant creak, surrendered to his unstoppable will and, like some massive prehistoric animal, came thundering down on him. For minutes he fought with the lumbering Victorian monstrosity, then sprang up jauntily from the floor, dusting his hands.

'It's all right!' he announced, eyeing the empty wardrobe. 'He's gone! You're all safe!'

There was a last crash as the wardrobe, breathing its last, fell to the floor, conceding defeat.

'Oh! Bravo!' cried the guests, and began to clap.

'Thank you, Captain Crummond,' Miss Roberts said warmly and graciously, shaking the hand of Britain's most decorated war hero. He kissed it gallantly and placed an arm round Rosemary's waist, causing her to sigh and giggle, her delicate tinkling blending prettily with the shingling sound as the last remaining wall mirror crashed to the floor and shattered into tiny pieces.

17

IN WHICH WE SEE THE RISE OF WORLD DESTRUCTION, THE GROWTH OF A MYTH, AND THE DECLINE AND FALL OF AN INFLATED LEGEND

THE PLIP-PLOP of dripping water could still be heard but, except for the spray of bullets in the walls and ceilings, no evidence remained of Captain Crummond's little skirmish with his elusive foe.

'So I was awarded the Victoria Cross,' he said modestly as he sat with Miss Fenton at the candlelit dining table, looking relaxed and debonair in an immaculate black dinner suit. 'But I can't take all the credit – there were one or two other chaps involved – a battalion, in fact!'

'You mean you did all that for England, and now you're risking your life for Daddy ... my Daddy?'

'And for you ... Rosemary.'

'Oh ... Hugh.'

Rosemary was quite overcome and could not hide the admiration in her eyes for the way in which he had stopped at nothing to protect the lives, property and peaceful serenity of these good, fine people. Modestly he brushed it aside, turning the conversation to her recent encounter with the von Brunnos.

'From what you've told me, Rosemary,' he said at last, 'you've done jolly well on your own.' He took her hand and gazed boldly into the twin lagoons of her eyes.

'In fact,' he added with sparkling generosity, 'a chap like me could very easily think about spending the rest of his life with a girl like you.'

Rosemary sighed and blushed like a beetroot salad, melted into mayonnaise, squeezed her legs like a sandwich, and squirmed and wriggled like a hungry caterpillar who'd just spotted its dinner.

'Oh… Could you, Hugh?' Her voice was wet, chewed-up lettuce, with a sprinkling of radish.

'But romantic notions will have to wait,' Bullshot said, as a waiter cleared away the remains of their dinner. 'We have some unfinished business. Perhaps you should give *me* the locket for safe keeping.'

'I gave it to the von Bwunnos,' she pointed out sadly.

'You *what?*' gasped Crummond, aghast – not for the first time nor the last – at feminine folly. 'Then we're *done* for.'

'No, you see, I took it—'

'No, don't apologise, Rosemary,' he interrupted wearily. 'After all, you are the weaker sex.'

'No, I—'

'Cripes,' Bullshot went on, 'what a *shambles* we'd be in if England were ever in the hands of a woman!'

'I'd taken the formula out of the locket and weplaced it with my scone wecipe,' she finally managed to explain.

Crummond was quite taken aback. 'You did, eh?'

'And then I hid it in my—'

Hugh quickly took the hint and looked away.

'—underthings,' Rosemary admitted shyly.

Hugh Crummond played the game: after all, had he not captained the England cricket team for five successive years?

'I suppose I owe you an apology,' he murmured. 'Am I forgiven?' He proffered his little finger.

'Of course, Hugh,' she replied, coyly linking her own with his.

'I'm not used to a gal with such pluck,' he admitted magnanimously.

'I'm not used to a man like ... Hugh ... Cwummond.' She intoned the name as if it were that of some deity.

Bullshot nodded understandingly. 'I *am* one of a special breed, Rosemary,' he agreed, 'the kind of chap who would rather die penniless than see this proud British Empire fall into the hands of the enemy.'

Rosemary was spellbound. 'Is the Empire in gwave danger, Hugh?' she asked, wide-eyed.

He became deadly serious. 'There are dark forces that besiege us at every turn,' he said gravely. 'The Bolshevik, the Levantine and the Proletariat. There is a world we must fight to preserve, Rosemary – where the Englishman reigns supreme, a being above all others, touched by destiny.'

As he spoke he became charged with the majesty of his rhetoric, rising from the table so that the stirring words could roam freely, resound and resonate across the Empire. Such was the power of his oratory that diners at nearby tables gathered around to listen and admire his statesmanship.

'A boy scout of the globe,' he went on, with three fingers of his right hand to his forehead in the famous salute. Fired with enthusiasm his performance became three-dimensional, with the magnetism and flourish of a consummate thespian. '... using the magnificence given to him by God's grace to bend nations before him—'

He bared his teeth and, to Rosemary's alarm, bent a teaspoon backwards between his clenched fists.

'—until this proud Empire stretches from pole—' he roared the word like a lion, puffed out his cheeks like an east wind, blew out his chest like a British bulldog '—to poooolle!'

His voice was cracking with emotion. Old ladies were dabbing their eyes with their handkerchiefs, the old colonel weeping uncontrollably, But Rosemary's eyes were growing goggly with alarm. It seemed to her that Hugh was acting a little strangely. Was it her imagination or was there a green tinge to his skin? And why was he sweating so profusely?

'Are you sure that spider didn't bite you, Hugh?'

'*Spider*!' thundered Bullshot, his cheeks inflated like balloons. '*What spider*!' His lips curled back in a hideous grimace and he was foaming at the mouth.

'When Daddy discovered the antidote a few years ago, he descwibed the symptoms to me.'

'REALLY!' Crummond screamed in a bloodcurdling, earsplitting roar that awoke guests from their beds, armchairs or brandies. 'WHAT ARE THEY?'

Beads of sweat dripped from his forehead and he was jerkily saluting. His skin had turned sea-green.

'Oh,' she replied matter-of-factly, 'delusions of gwandeur, wanting and waving—'

'WANTING AND WAVING?'

'No ... *wanting* and *waving*,' Rosemary corrected him.

'OH RANTING AND RAVING!'

'Yes and sweating of the forehead, constant saluting, green complexion ... all the usual things. The most telltale clue is—'

There was a loud, ripping noise.

'—swelling of the extwemities!' She finished, throwing up her hands in horror: the sleeve of his black dinner jacket was visibly inflating.

'BLAST!' he boomed, as the arm burst through the seam. 'MY TAILOR ALWAYS MAKES THE DAMN SLEEVES TOO TIGHT!'

The sleeve ripped to the shoulder, his wristwatch warped and exploded, shooting springs and wheels everywhere, and his shirt buttons pooped open.

Rosemary almost fainted at the sight of his white vest. 'Hugh!' she cried desperately, 'that spider *did* bite you, didn't it?'

'*Probably*,' admitted the Captain as he shot up from his seat.

'But its bite is fatal!' she protested anxiously.

'PROBABLY,' he snorted.

'It would kill an avewage man in seconds!' she warbled in fright.

With an impact that made the walls of the inn shiver and shake, Hugh Crummond stamped his swollen foot on the floor.

'I'M NOT ... AVERAGE!' he thundered.

The next moment, his body now bloated to the size of a small barrage balloon, he collapsed backwards on the floor.

PART 2

Bullshot
Crummond
Bounces
Back

18

I N THE FOUL STENCH and squalor of the Black Baron of Blitzburg's torture chamber deep in the malignant bowels of Netherington Manor, Professor Rupert Fenton, world-famous scientist and Hun hostage, was reaching the end of his tether. He stared with astonishment at the two pieces of paper on the workbench next to his daughter's locket.

'How did you get the other half of the formula?' he waffled. 'What have you done to my daughter?'

The laughter of his tormentors was like ditchwater. Lenya swatted a hornet against her bosom, while at the same time catching a passing fly and a feeding it to the Venus flytrap that adorned one shoulder of her black gown.

'Your daughter saw reason and so must you,' barked the Count. 'I have provided you viz everyzing you need to carry out zis experiment, right down to ze eggs.'

'Eggs?' echoed the egghead, unable to believe his ears. 'Let me see that formula.'

Von Brunno handed him the two sheets of paper and he turned away to study them while Crouch, coughing up gobs of phlegm, shuffled towards them with a tray of buzzards' eggs. He barged into the workbench on which a cornucopia of scientific equipment had been installed: eggs rolled off the tray, cracking on the floor, their faint putrescent odour quickly gobbled up by the vile miasma.

A smile flickered over the scientist's face as he recognised his daughter's scone recipe, but he concealed his excitement.

'All right, von Brunno,' he acceded. 'You leave me no choice.'

The Professor began to select ingredients from the bench. 'Now, let me see ... eight tablespoons of flour, one egg...'

Scientifically he broke the egg into a mixing basin and threw the wet shells carelessly over his shoulder: they splattered against the monocle of the Count, who wiped the muck off the lens in grim silence.

'... A pinch of sodium chloride, carbonate of soda...'

'It is a pleasure to see you so co-operative, Professor,' observed the Count.

'Nonsense!' replied the Professor, cheerfully stirring the dough with a wooden spoon. 'You know I can't resist a little chemistry for long. Now for the heating process. We'll need to heat this for half an hour at 350 degrees Fahrenheit – or Gas Mark Four ...'

He looked up and gazed fixedly and with utter sincerity at the intrigued Count.

'Von Brunno – you are witnessing the creation of one of the hardest substances known to man.'

'Have one of my home-made scones, Dobbs,' Rosemary chirped happily as she flitted around her familiar parlour in a frilly, white apron. 'They're Daddy's favouwites.'

She joined the manservant at the sitting-room table. Her father's grandfather clock chimed the quarter hour and from the garden came the soothing buzz of the ancient family retainer's lawnmower.

'Oh, very kind of you, Miss,' replied Dobbs gratefully. He bit into the scone and winced in pain as a sliver of bone flaked from a tooth.

'Ah! Early morning tea!' Captain Crummond announced heartily from the doorway, looking rather dazed as he strode over to the table and performed his chest-expanding exercises.

'No, Hugh,' replied Rosemary sweetly, 'elevenses. *You've* been sleeping off the spider antidote.'

'Impossible!' he snapped as though any further discussion on the matter was completely out of the question, then stopped, like a dog who had just sniffed a rabbit. He looked around the room and raised his eyebrow with an air of cunning.

'Wait a moment,' he warned them and, darting to the window, scrutinised the vast lawns of the Elms estate. 'This is *not* the Whippet Inn!' He swivelled round to survey the effect on them of this shattering piece of news.

'No, sir,' replied his valet patiently. 'This is Miss Fenton's place. We brought you 'ere last night when you was green and unconscious.'

Bullshot was taken aback. 'Why didn't you wake me?' he said indignantly. 'The von Brunnos will be streets ahead of us now – and who knows where?'

'I think *I* do, Hugh,' Rosemary replied with a hint of smugness as the handed him a scone. 'I've been doing a *little* detective work myself. With von Bwunno's umbwella handle fwom the twain!'

Crummond crossed to the window and peered inside a large Chinese urn: it was full of scones from previous mealtimes. Surreptitiously he dropped his little rock on top of the others.

'The label weads "Tweadaway and Harbottle, Little Nethewington", she read, and wheeled round in triumph. 'That's the village where Aunt Josephine lives.'

Bullshot sighed wearily. 'What is all this leading to, Rosemary?' was what he meant to say but unfortunately, due to the rock-hard lump of concrete that by now seemed to have taken permanent residence in his mouth, the words came out sounding like 'Wha-i-iaw-i-ee-i-oo-o-a-ee?'

'Well, I telephoned her and she said that some foweign-looking people had just moved into old Nethewington Manor.'

She began to prowl across the room just like detectives did when they were thinking.

As she did so, Bullshot took the opportunity to nip across to the sofa and add his scone to a very large pile of similar scones hidden under a cushion. This historic pile, for which the Professor had presumably laid the foundation stone, had no doubt been added to by many visitors over the years. Dobbs meanwhile, as befitted his role, neatly pocketed his scone inside his waistcoat and by the time Rosemary had turned, master and servant were both back in place.

'I know the Manor,' she went on, 'nobody has lived there since I was a gal.'

'That *is* a long time,' Bullshot agreed, not appearing to notice when she bridled slightly. 'Perhaps I should get over there and ferret around a little.' He made for the door.

'Hold your 'orses, guv'nor,' said Dobbs. 'If it is the von Brunnos and you fall into their 'ands, they'll torture you to extract the formula.'

Crummond shook his head sagely. 'I have the advantage of them. I know nothing.'

'But when will they wealise that you know nothing?' protested Rosemary.

'When I'm dead,' he replied as if it were obvious.

'How will we know if you're dead, sir?' asked Dobbs.

'If I'm not back in time for tea,' Bullshot replied with a hint of intrigue.

'Oh, Hugh. Do be careful,' Rosemary gasped.

But it was too late – he was gone.

19

In Which Bullshot is Fooled by a French Widow and Crouch is Foul by a French Window

Captain Crummond squatted in the shrubbery behind a semi-circular balustrade, his trusty binoculars revealing the sinister pointed towers of Netherington Manor. He popped his pipe into the corner of his mouth and, without removing his eyes from the binoculars, climbed over the balustrade and darted nimbly forward.

From behind a bush, Countess Lenya von Brunno, dressed in a flowering dress that did little to disguise the voluptuous curves of her statuesque body, coolly observed the Englishman in his tweed jacket and short trousers as he steadily moved towards the gothic pile. Suddenly he seemed to sink down; amusement flickered on her scarlet lips as she saw that he had stepped into a small ornamental pond containing a statue.

She turned on a tap: a fountain gushed from the statue. drenching him and knocking him back into the pond. She smiled again, and stepped from the bushes.

'Good afternoon,' she purred in a French accent.

'Good afternoon,' Bullshot spluttered, '… er … I'm on a walking tour of England. Could I trouble you for a glass of water?'

Her lips curled once more in ironic amusement. 'No need to drink from that filthy fountain,' she replied

BULLSHOT

archly. 'Come up to ze house and have a glass of Vichy.'

For a sneaking moment Hugh Crummond was tempted to regard himself as though he were a man and to regard her as though she were a woman; then he remembered that he had more important things to attend to.

'Wait a moment,' he said, struck by a thought. 'You mean, this is *your* house?'

She smiled. 'But of course,' she replied huskily.

'I'm sorry, but I understood it was recently occupied by sinister *foreign* types.'

'I am French,' she said throatily. 'Do you find me so sinister?'

Crummond's cheeks turned red and he chortled with embarrassment. 'Certainly not.'

She took his hand. 'I am Mrs Yvette Platt-Higgins.'

'And I am Captain Hugh Crummond,' he replied

gamely.

'Oh!' she said, putting her hand to her throat. 'But you are famous!'

Bullshot laughed modestly. 'I have a certain reputation,' he said, offering her his arm as they walked towards the mansion.

Through an upstairs window Count Otto von Brunno observed the little scene as Crouch danced sluglike attendance on him.

'So,' he chuckled. 'Crummond has taken ze bait. Soon ze meddling fool of an Englishmen will be out of my hair!'

Behind him, Crouch rolled his yellowing eyes towards his master's bald head and grimaced like a gargoyle.

'So, Mrs Platt-Higgins,' Bullshot remarked conversation-lly as she poured him a brandy in the library. 'What first attracted you to these parts?'

His short, tweed trousers, drenched from being soaked in the fountain, appeared to have shrunk somewhat so that they now clung tightly to his crotch. As he stood before her, hands behind his back and legs akimbo, Lenya von Brunno turned to regard those particular parts with evident interest for a lingering moment, then turned back to the drinks cabinet. 'I am ze widow of ze late Colonel Platt-Heegins of ze Sussex Fusiliers.'

'I know them well,' he replied as she handed him his brandy.

'I met him when I was a nurse in France. We married but unhappily his war wounds prevented him from doing certain things.'

Crummond was only too familiar with the problem. 'A lot of chaps couldn't hunt after the war,' he said sympathetically.

'He died ten years ago. I have been … alone in this house ever since.' A tear seemed to fall.

'If it's any consolation, Madam,' offered Hugh, 'the Sussex Fusiliers were a damn fine regiment.'

'Thank you, Captain Crumm—' She gasped as her hand made contact with the top of his V-necked pullover beneath the tightly buttoned jacket. 'You will, perhaps, stay for dinner.'

'Most kind, but no,' Bullshot replied, shaking his head. He leaned forward confidentially. '*Entre nous*, I'm on a case.'

She giggled and put a finger to her lips conspiratorially.

'I'm helping a Miss Fenton to find her kidnapped father,' he explained.

Lenya had her back to Crummond; for an instant a look of pure venom flashed across her enticing face, then it was gone.

'I understand,' she purred. 'But you will at least allow me to get you into a hot bath…'

'It's getting late,' said Rosemary, pacing nervously about the living room. 'I hope Hugh's not in danger.'

'Don't worry, Miss,' replied Dobbs. 'The Captain's been in hot water before.'

Through a chink in the bedroom wall Lenya von Brunno was observing with drooling pleasure the spectacle of Captain Crummond, pipe in mouth but otherwise naked and defenceless, as he performed his ablutions in the bath tub whose overflow aperture constituted the other end of the fiendish telescope.

'So Miss Fenton is still alive!' concluded the Count, dragging on a cheroot through an ivory holder and ambling up and down the bedroom in his elegant dark velvet smoking jacket. 'And she has ze other half of ze formula!'

'With Crummond here, she is unprotected,' replied Lenya, draped on a chaise longue in a careless transparent negligée. 'You must get it at once.'

'Impossible!' snapped von Brunno. 'I must attend ze symposium in London.'

'Then arrange for Miss Fenton to meet you there,' ordered the German woman.

'How?'

Lenya's eyes were blazing daggers. 'Vocal reiteration,' she hissed.

'Excellent!' crowed the Black Baron of Blirzburg.

'I will stay here and dispose of Captain Crummond.'

'No,' said the Count. 'That pleasure will be mine.' He had not forgotten their last encounter on the summit of Mount Kanchenjunga when Bullshot had thwarted his plan to turn the human race into an ordered hierarchy of zombies, enslaved by his will. 'You detain him until I return.'

'But this is our chance to eliminate him and—' She peered once more through the overflow aperture. Captain Crummond, holding his loofah firmly in front of his intimate region, was about to climb out of the bath.

When, after an unconscionably long time, she turned back to the Count, there was a salacious glint in her eye.

'You are right, Otto,' she sighed deeply and lasciviously. 'I will detain ze *prominent* Captain.'

In the Stygian dungeon of Netherington Manor, Professor Fenton was sitting bound to a chair, struggling to free himself. Muffled groans could be heard from his gagged mouth. But the scientist could not avoid observing with clinical curiosity the fiendish contraption before him – it looked damnably complicated, dastardly clever and disgustingly lethal.

'Back! Down! In!' ordered the Count, and then with a sigh of triumph, 'Modulate!' He picked up a prepared script.

At his control panel, Crouch hooked his fungoid finger on to a telephone dial...

The servile Crouch sat at a control panel, pimpled with dozens of knobs. From this a tangle of wires snaked to a metal frame into which the Count was harnessed. A metal arm with a moving metal hand and spiky fingers was also wired to the control panel and at a series of commands from the Count to Crouch it protracted itself and wheeled round to grip the Count's Adam's apple. This, then, was the vocal reiteration machine.

'Horsted Keynes two thwee...' came Rosemary's anxious voice through a horn wired to a diabolical sound-amplification machine.

'Hello ... Rosemary ... dear,' the Count read into another horn. The voice was unmistakably that of Professor Fenton, though lower, gruffer and punctuated by unnatural pauses.

'Daddy!' squeaked Rosemary excitedly.

'I'm ... perfectly ... safe,' the Count recited.

Crouch monitored the operation with ghastly glee while the Professor himself, as if having his tooth extracted, remained bound to his chair, forced to suffer through this travesty, this cruel deception.

'Oh, wonderful!' Miss Fenton trilled.

'I'm ... sorry ... to ... upset ... you ... dear ... but ... I've ... been ... working .... undercover. I'll ... explain ... everything ... when ... I ... see ... you. Now ... I ... want ... you ... the ... formula ... to ... London ... bring.'

'To London the formula bwing?' Rosemary suggested, puzzled. 'Daddy, are you all wight?'

'Of ... course ... I'm ... all ... right,' said the Count.

But something was definitely going wrong. The voice was slowing perceptibly.

'Meet ... me ... at ... the Symposium ... of ... Scientific ... Discoverers.'

There was no doubt about it: the machine was malfunctioning, like a 78 rpm record being played at 16 rpm. The Count signalled frantically at Crouch, who gurgled as he tried to adjust the controls.

'Daddy, I can't understand you.' She shook the receiver to correct the fault.

'Iiieee … ssaaiidd … mmeeeett … mmeee … aattt … thhee … Ssssyymmppoossiiuummm … ooff … Scientific … *Discovers!*'

For a few moments the voice returned to normal.

'I … shall … be … speaking … in … the … Sir … Isaac … Newton … Room. It's-essential-*that-you're-there.*' The voice was now speeding up.

Crouch dithered with the knobs as if having an epileptic seizure and the metal hand around the Count's throat went into spasms.

'*IshallbespeakingintheSirIsaacNewtonRoomItsessentialthat yourethelshlbspkgithsisntnrmthlyth…*'

'Daddy, have you been overworking again?' Rosemary asked indulgently. 'Now keep calm … Don't fwet, I'll be there.'

She hung up with a sigh of relief.

The Count was writhing in agony as the metal fingers closed ever more tightly on his vocal cords. The gabbling increased in speed until it became a continuous high-pitched whine.

As Crouch wrestled with the controls the machine began to belch clouds of thick purple smoke. Just before the metal hand would have snapped his vocal cords and severed his neck arteries, the Count yanked it off his throat. With an almighty explosion, the infernal machine blew up.

20

In Which the Captain Mounts a Rescue and Lenya Mounts the Captain

'Hope you enjoyed your bath, Captain,' Countess Lenya von Brunno enquired of her guest, her slinky form basking in the glow from the fireplace, where she posed monumentally, like a love goddess in a picture palace, at the same time as being poised voraciously, like a piranha in a paddling pool.

Hugh Crummond stumbled into the room in an oversized black silk dressing gown that trailed behind him like a peacock's tail, singly disquieted by its fresh cologne smell, considering the fact that Colonel Platt-Higgins had been deceased for a decade, but doubly disconcerted when he clapped eyes on the Colonel's widow: the shamelessly low-cut silver-lamé dress under the gossamer-thin black-lace gown left little to the imagination; what *was* left was totally tantalising.

Bullshot clenched his fists: this was going to be rather tricky.

'Wonderfully invigorating, thank you,' he said politely.

Lenya wriggled towards him. 'Would you...' She indicated wordlessly for him to divest her of her wispy wrapping. He obliged.

'Help yourself to some more cognac,' she added.

She undulated towards an ornate gramophone,

suggestively bending to wind it up before slipping a
Duke Ellington record on the turntable.

'Do you like ze new American jazz?' she purred.

'Hate it,' he replied primly. 'It leaves me quite cold.'

He turned from the drinks cabinet and flushed hotly,
his eyes bulging; the silver-lamé décolletage so
audaciously revealing in front was positively indecent
from behind, plunging well below the waist and
wickedly exposing the cleft of her derrière.

'I adore it,' she sighed. 'It makes me feel like a
woman.' She writhed sensually to the shockingly
decadent Negro music, pressing herself back against a
sofa, displaying to Hugh's embarrassment her shapely
profile as she continued her mincing movements.

He could stand it no longer. 'Is this *seemly*, Mrs Platt-Higgins?' he protested. 'Playing *popular* music, and your husband only *ten* years dead?'

Grinding her hips, she slunk towards him. 'I find it arouses ze most *savage* passions,' she whispered sensuously, running her hand up Captain Crummond's chest and around his neck.

'Yes, it's absolutely bestial,' he agreed distastefully.

'Mmm, what strong shoulders you have, Captain,' she murmured, caressing them as she clamped him in her boa constrictor embrace.

'I say,' he spluttered, 'is it getting a trifle close in here, or what?'

'Yes, yes, you're right,' she gasped, stroking his cheek and rubbing her body against him. She allowed herself to fall back in his arms. 'I feel ... faint. Help me to ze chaise-longue.'

Obediently, but with rather more effort than he had imagined necessary, he lifted Lenya, whose arms were still draped around his neck, to the chaise-longue where, arching her back, she stretched herself seductively.

'My fan,' she sighed.

Crummond picked up a fat, white, feathery fan and used it to cool her own perspiring person, while the vixen carefully arranged herself to expose most of her shapely legs. She began to breathe deeply and throatily, heaving her bosom, as if in the throes of a fever.

'What is it?' he asked in alarm as he rushed to kneel at her side. 'A seizure? Don't panic! Military training teaches a chap how to revive the unconscious.' He leaned across her, placing his hands on her heaving breasts. 'Now a little artificial respiration,' he snapped briskly, kneading them like moist dough.

'Aaaaghh! Aaaaaghh!' Lenya squirmed ecstatically, eyes rolling, tongue lolling, as she revelled in the heat of her Hunnish she-devil passion.

'Sorry,' said Bullshot busily. 'Have to be cruel to be kind.' Without pause, he pressed his hands down in slow, rhythmic, pumping movements.

Lenya went wild, locking her arms and thighs around him, moaning and groaning deliriously. Still locked in her embrace, Bullshot suddenly found her towering above him as she lifted herself from the sofa and, in one convulsive movement, rolled him on to her tiger skin rug. Pinning him on his back to the ground, she sat astride his hips and rode him.

With superhuman human effort, Captain Crummond managed to roll himself round until he was on top of her, only to feel her raised thigh locking itself around his.

This was really going too far.

'*Mrs Platt-Higgins!*' he exploded.

But Lenya had now gained enough leverage to roll him onto his back again, this time arching him back directly over the tiger's head. As she did so, the slit in her skirt rode up above her silk stockings, revealing a tattoo on the creamy flesh of the inside of her thigh.

'Ha!' he exclaimed, as the hideous truth dawned. 'The von Brunno family crest! You're no war widow, you're Lenya von Brunno.'

'Vot do you care?' cried Lenya, too far gone in her lecherous designs to turn back. 'Make love to me, you fool!'

She rode him with yet more fury, moaning and groaning yet more greedily.

'This is all an infernal ruse!' Crummond complained, sitting up on his elbows and levering himself backwards towards the door as Lenya, still riding him, approached her climax. 'And Rosemary must be in danger.'

Like an industrious badger, he tunnelled his way out from under the Jezebel, and jumped to his feet. Lenya, still astride but with nothing between her legs, lunged at the departing train of his dressing gown, bringing the stoked and charging engine that was Hugh Crummond crashing to the ground.

He jumped up once again and vanished puffing through the door, leaving the Countess Lenya von Brunno to paw and clutch at the empty floor, seething with frustration, while the evil jazz music played on.

Still in the Count's lofty robe, Bullshot hooted and screeched his black Lagonda to a halt in front of the Elms, just as Dobbs appeared in the gravel courtyard.

'Where's Rosemary?' he demanded.

'Gone to meet her father, guv'nor,' replied the valet.

'Her father!'

'Yes, he telephoned. He said, "I want you to London the formula bring."'

'A split infinitive from an Oxford man?' said Crummond sceptically. 'Impossible. There's only one language that uses that construction with such annoying regularity—' he screwed up his face with loathing '— German!'

'Are you saying it was the von Brunnos, sir?'

'Using vocal reiteration,' Bullshot replied crisply. He opened the passenger door. 'Come along, Dobbs, there's not a moment to lose. We must rescue Rosemary at once.'

The manservant was appalled. 'Not dressed like that you won't, sir,' he insisted. 'I've laid out your Birdseye tweed, and there's a clean pair of underpants on the heater...'

With a sigh, Hugh Crummond obeyed. In matters of dress, it is always most prudent to defer to one's valet.

21

IN WHICH DR BLITZER'S BEEP IS BLOWN BY ALBERT EINSTEIN, THE BLACK BARON'S BAMBOOZLE IS BLOWN BY MISS FENTON AND THE MOST BRILLIANT MINDS IN THE UNIVERSE ARE BLOWN BY A GIANT AEROSOL

T HE HEADQUARTERS of the Royal Society of Scientific Discovers was an imposing mid-Victorian building in the heart of South Kensington. Although one of the more obscure and esoteric products of Prince Albert's relentless quest to bring the universe to the hub of the Empire – to the greater glory of both – some of the most explosive and revolutionary scientific inventions of Modern Times had first been unveiled within its portals.

Hugh Crummond had himself received there some not unflattering comments and a modest measure of immortality, through one or two of his own little offerings – his Underwater Shooting Umbrella had not only established itself as a technical classic of subaquatic engineering but had also made a decent contribution towards the safety of the human race in fishing up the abominable Scandinavian Midget out of his icy hiding hole deep below the murky waters of the Skaggerak.

In the high-windowed lecture theatre, with its august pillars and vast chandeliers, Dr Eugene Blitzer, the eccentric Boston boffin, was demonstrating his latest invention, an enormous machine that had taken a morning for him to devise, assemble and test, and another fourteen years to iron out a single, peculiar operating hitch – namely a strategically timed response signal.

However, within the last four years had come the long-awaited breakthrough and now the Blitzerian Electrically Emitted Pulse – or BEEP – had been trapped, tested, tuned, retested, piloted, perfected and patented. The world was now ready for its maiden emission.

'The Telephone,' he drawled after a smattering of applause from the distinguished company of inventors and scientists. 'Many times it will ring when you are out and you wanna know who called. Hence the "Telephone Answering Machine" – an apparatus that will enable you to respond to telephonic communication in absentia.'

He beamed owlishly and pressed a button. The loud, tinny voice of Dr Blitzer himself crackled from the large horn that protruded from the main carriage of the apparatus. The machine started to whine and wink with flashing lights in various places.

'*Hi, this is Eugene and Sandy Blitzer!*' answered the machine telephonically in a bland, amiable tone. '*We're not home right now, but leave a message after the beep and we'll get right back to you.*'

Dr Blitzer wandered round the machine as it spoke, smiling contentedly at the gathering. The whine continued – but there was no beep.'

'Zere is no beep,' ventured a German scientist with a shock of white hair and a thick moustache. The assembly glared disapprovingly at Dr Albert Einstein, but Dr Blitzer seemed genuinely mortified.

'I am still, er, working on the beep,' he apologised.

Politely the assembly applauded as the machine continued to whine and wink.

'Thank you, Dr Blitzer,' said the Chairman, who had led the clapping. 'Now gentlemen, we are very honoured to have with us this evening Professor Rupert Fenton.'

A tall, gaunt figure, bearing the unmistakable hallmarks of the Professor's trifocals and unkempt hair, arose from a bench and moved towards the podium. 'Gentlemen,' he announced hoarsely. 'Please gather round as I am suffering from laryngitis.'

The scientists nodded sympathetically and left their benches to crowd round him in a circle, looking curiously at the gigantic canister.

'I would like to demonstrate my new invention, which I call ze Gaseous Particle Propellant.'

As he spoke a young woman dressed in white was entering the lecture hall; as she walked the length of its centre aisle a suspicious frown began to form on her delicate Anglo Saxon features.

'It is a multi-utilitarian device depending on ze nature of its content,' continued the speaker. 'Note, when I depress lever "A", a fine spray is emitted through nozzle "B"—' he began to demonstrate.

'*You're not Daddy!*' Rosemary Fenton screamed.

Heads turned to see who was responsible for this disorderly interjection. Unconcerned, Rosemary rushed to the podium to confront the speaker, but he had the advantage. He aimed the fiendish canister at Miss Fenton and depressed the plunger: a fine spray covered the entire assembly – and principally Rosemary.

'You're Otto von—' she just had time to gasp before stumbling onto a bench next to Dr Blitzer.

By now the whole enclave of eggheads was collapsing in gales of effervescent guffaws, over which Rosemary's high-pitched giggle soared like a demented obbligato in a flute concerto.

'What's in the can?' piped Dr Blitzer in helpless glee.

'A very exotic drug from Asia,' declared the imposter, removing his moustache, wig and bifocals, 'commonly called Indian hemp, or...' he inserted his monocle and the abominable Count Otto von Brunno rose like a towering inferno above the heads of the befuddled boffins, '*Marijuana!*'

'Interesting,' chortled Dr Blitzer, drooling at the mouth. 'It induces extreme lethargy and euphoria. And unbridled lechery.'

His owlish grin manic with lust, he lasciviously slipped his hand along Miss Fenton's thigh. Prostrate in his arms and lap, she was too hysterical to notice or care, and her only response was to screech with delirious laughter.

'In less than fifty years, Dr Blitzer,' the Count crowed triumphantly, 'I predict that this drug will incapacitate an entire generation!'

Amidst the uproar, Crouch lumbered in like a bloated baby elephant in a gas mask with a long trunk-like hose, pushing two bulky laundry wicker baskets. With a wicked gleam in his monocle von Brunno opened them, lifted the giggling squithering body of Rosemary Fenton in his arms and looked about him triumphantly.

'All ze Vorld's knowledge – and Miss Fenton too!' he shrieked and, laughing the laughter of Beelzebub, handed her to Crouch, who flopped her like a slithery goldfish into one of the baskets, where she continued to screech deliriously.

22

In Which an Extraordinary Theory Sticks in Dr Einstein's Throat,
an Explosive Fury Sticks in Captain Crummond's Mouth
and an Excruciating Flunkey is Stuck on Miss Fenton's Feet

THE BLACK BARON of Blitzburg and the loathsome
lackey Crouch loaded the cornucopia of contraptions,
the agglomeration of gadgets, the stockpile of the
most intricate scientific inventions, the fruits of an
entire lifetime's knowledge of the greatest minds of the
nineteenth and twentieth centuries, into the laundry
baskets, along with Miss Fenton, and wheeled them
swiftly into the Institute washroom, leaving the
incapacitated eggheads to their demented ramblings and
ravings.

Crouch stumbled to the window to check that their
imminent departure in the Mercedes would not be
obstructed. Through the dreadful sties that clouded his
vision he could make out a car, an open tourer driving at
more than twice the speed of other traffic, approaching
the Institute and pulling to a halt with a squeal of brakes.
An immaculately attired gentleman in Birdseye tweed
jumped out of the black Lagonda and raced into the
building.

'Wait here, Dobbs!' he called out to his trusty servant.
'If I'm not back in five minutes, you know what to do.'

With the haste of a mound of lichen Crouch shuffled

up to his tormentor and pointed, drivelling and coughing incoherently.

'Crummond!' exclaimed the Count in a flash. 'What? Lenya allowed him to escape?'

Crouch made a noise like lumpy soup slowly disappearing down a kitchen sink waste pipe.

'Do not panic!' von Brunno snapped, inserting his monocle. 'There must be something here we can use.'

He delved into the laundry baskets, roughly pushing Miss Fenton aside. The baskets tipped over, sending Rosemary and the scientific inventions cascading across the washroom floor. The giant telephone answering machine was instantly triggered into action.

'*Hi, this is Eugene and Sandy Blitzer! ... Hi, this is Eugene and Sandy Blitzer! ... Hi, this is Eugene and Sandy Blitzer! ... Hi, this is Eugene and Sandy Blitz—*'

With a grunt Crouch picked up the machine and smashed it to the floor. It whined and winked for a few moments, then fizzled out.

'Aha!' exclaimed the Count, extracting an infernal-looking device from the harvest of inventions heaped around the floor. 'A Converse Force Field! It can be used for Good—' he turned malevolently to his slave, and grinned '—or Evil!'

Captain Hugh 'Bullshot' Crummond, DSO, MC & Bar, late of His Majesty's Loamshires and Royal Flying Corps, sprinted into the lecture hall with the speed of an Olympic champion and stopped dead as he registered the supine forms, crazed countenances and giggling cacophony.

One scientist with waxed, pointed moustache was sitting piggy-back on another, who was attempting to waltz.

'Great Scott!' exclaimed Bullshot. 'It's Doctor Giuseppe Perotti ... and Dr Hans Ulbricht from Zurich...'

He moved hastily to a third scientist with a white shock of hair and thick moustache, who was chewing up a sheet of paper that read $E = mc^2$. 'And Doctor er ...' but the man was a relative stranger.

Another scientist with a demented owlish grin was writhing on the floor with an elderly female physicist who was screaming.

'Dr Eugene Blitzer! What are you doing?' Crummond gasped.

Suddenly it all became clear to him. 'Good heavens!' he exclaimed. 'You've all been doped! The finest minds of our generation turned to mush!'

But the distant piercing scream of Miss Rosemary Fenton distracted him from his diatribe. He raced for the door and ran full pelt down the corridor, then froze as the full horror of her fate dawned on him.

'Rosemary!' he exclaimed. 'In the gentlemen's washroom! Oh no!' He burst through the door to discover Miss Fenton lolloping on the floor, her arms propped up against a laundry basket. She was giggling happily.

'Yoo hoo, Hugh,' giggled Rosemary, throwing her white glove flirtatiously into his nose.

'Are you safe?' he cried urgently, rushing to kneel by her side.

'Quite safe with me, Captain Crummond!' growled the Black Baron of Blitzburg.

Hugh Crummond wheeled round to face his deadly

adversary, but for once his lightning reflexes were not quite quick enough. For the Count was brandishing in his arms the fiendish Converse Force Field machine and he instantly pressed its button: a deadly ray of searing blue light shot out into the Captain's path. Sparks flew from Crummond's head, chest, arms and legs, and his hair stood on end.

'Aaargh! Aaargh!' he managed to gasp through a mouth that had turned to granite. 'What the devil's going on?'

The evil blue ray hovered in the space between the two of them, and slowly lengthened as the Count's vicious device forced the Captain's inexorable retreat against the wall.

'This is a Converse Force Field!' von Brunno announced with a smile. 'One of many new toys now in my possession.'

'You won't get away with this, you know,' was what Bullshot wanted to say, but it came out as a monotonous gurgle:

'*A ging ga goo!*'

'It's no use trying to speak,' von Brunno replied evenly as Crouch once more loaded the floppy Miss Fenton into one of the laundry baskets. 'You are now totally paralysed. And what is more, ze first person through that door will cause an Inverse Force Field, thus reversing ze polarities...'

He reached into his pocket and pulled out a long cigar-shaped object. 'And causing this stick of dynamite to explode!'

He clamped the explosive between Crummond's clenched teeth.

'Yoo hoo, Hugh!' sang Rosemary from the laundry basket, which Crouch wheeled out of the washroom.

The Hun took a last look at his erstwhile enemy. 'Goodbye, Captain Crummond,' he laughed maliciously.

Down the corridor lurched Crouch with the laundry baskets bearing Rosemary and the means to rule the universe, followed by the Count, rubbing his hands with grim satisfaction. Turning the corner he bumped into a gentleman dressed in a valet's uniform.

'The Captain?' asked Dobbs anxiously.

The Count paused, then smiled evilly. 'He's in ze washroom,' he called out over his shoulder as he scurried down the steps.

Dobbs frowned, puzzled. The Captain had been gone for five and a quarter minutes. He knew what to do. He moved down the corridor until he reached the washroom, and then hesitated, his hand closing on the door handle.

'Are you in there, Captain?' he called out.

Inside the washroom Captain Crummond widened his eyes in terror, knowing full well that the Count's was no idle threat and that his own manservant, as reliable as the Rock of Gibraltar, was about to blow him to Kingdom Come.

The handle slowly turned...

As if in some tremulous response to this awesome moment in the history of this world, a faint but distinct pulse, like a primeval heartbeat, was emitted from the washroom floor.

Dr Blitzer's brainchild had begun to beep...

23

THE SLEEK BLACK Mercedes sped silently through the night, its evil occupants now convinced that nothing and no one could thwart their diabolical enterprise.

In the back seat Miss Rosemary Fenton leaned, mercifully unconscious, on the crooked shoulder of the Black Baron of Blitzburg, who, with a greedy glint in his monocle, was untying the strings of her chaste cape to steal the most precious thing she possessed, hidden in her underthings...

Suddenly he ceased his lewd manipulations as in the driving mirror he observed the horrible visage of his lackey, tongue lolling with the lascivious expectation of a habitual voyeur. The Count pulled down the blind, obscuring the proceedings from his drooling driver. The cretinous smirk on the mute's mouth was instantly replaced by its habitual scowl. Seconds later the blind flew up again: Crouch grinned like a gargoyle. The Count again pulled down the blind and at the wheel Crouch fumed sullenly.

The Count renewed his endeavours, sliding his hand down the virginal white cotton brassiere. With a wicked leer he began to rummage inside. The Englishwoman stirred and, without opening her eyes, smiled contentedly and giggled, the last lingering effects of the potent drug reawakening her euphoria.

'Oh ... mm,' she murmured drowsily. 'Ahhhh ... that tickles...'

With a grunt of triumph the Count at last plucked the piece of paper with the formula from her brassiere, and dropped it in his pocket. Then he returned to Miss Fenton's breasts. The poor deluded lady ran her fingers across the head of her father's tormentor and with devious delight he responded to her innocent advances as she caressed the smooth, hairless dome.

Suddenly her eyes popped open, goggly with horror, as she realised the horrible truth. She stared into his leering face and screamed with fright. The Count laughed like a maniac and in the front seat Crouch's mouth widened in a ghastly grin.

'Why have you brought ze girl?' Countess Lenya von Brunno demanded, as the Black Baron of Blitzburg swept into the entrance hall of Netherington Manor, followed by Crouch with Rosemary, gagged, slung over his shoulder like a sack of potatoes.

'Why did you let Crummond go?' parried the Count. 'You were under strict instruction from me to detain him.'

The scheming adulteress fell at the feet of her partner in crime. 'I tried,' she protested from the bottom of her black heart, 'but he was an animal; his hands were all over me.' She rubbed herself like a hungry cat against the Count's unbending body. 'His lips pressed against mine. He explored every part of my body.'

Rosemary covered her ears in disgust and Crouch started to sidle off with her, drooling and whimpering with anticipation.

'No doubt he stretched your capacity to resist beyond its breaking point!' snarled the Count.

'Oh yes, yes,' sighed Lenya, aroused by the memory.

'*And then you broke!*' screamed the Count, hurling her to the sofa.

'Oh no, no, Otto, *Liebchen*,' she moaned imploringly. 'You are ze only von in my life. It has always been you.'

'Let it remain so,' he acquiesced, holding his arm out to hers. 'Never forget that there is a bond of evil between us that can only be broken by ... *death!*' He lunged at her, burying his head in her viperfish bosom; she gasped with pleasure and triumph.

Suddenly Rosemary screamed. The Count turned to discover Crouch gluttonously pawing her on the chaise-longue.

'Ze girl,' Lenya reminded him.

'Of course,' the Count replied. 'Crouch!'

Instantly there was a loud clump, like the sound of a sack of potatoes falling. The lackey shuffled over to do his master's bidding, having deposited Miss Fenton on the floor.

'We depart at dawn!' announced the Count, looking once more into Lenya's treacherous eyes.

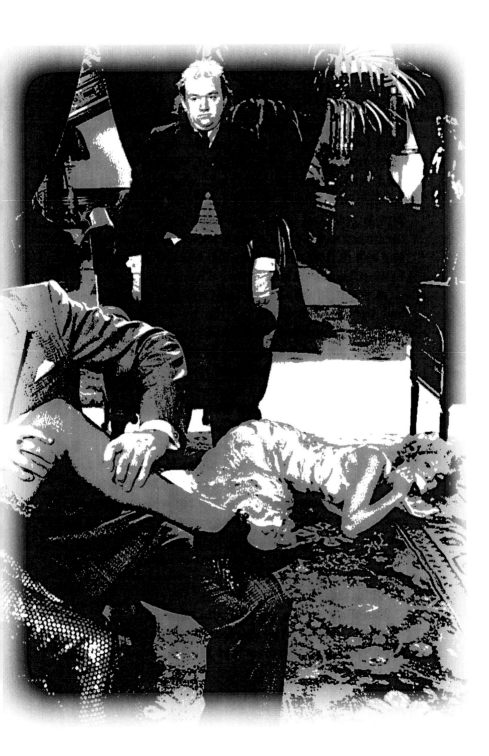

In the misty, eerie light of early dawn the clifftop could have been the setting for some Nordic saga, a place of myth and legend, goblin and fiend. Here lay purgatory, a land 'twixt Heaven and Hell, where acts of godly heroism and satanic devilry had been played out since time began. And to this cursed and blessed precipice on the Sussex coast came a black Mercedes that shuddered to a halt in front of a barrier that blocked a track leading to the edge of the cliff.

A young blonde-haired lady was led, gagged, bound and trembling, towards the rim by an oafish flunkey, while a tall, crooked man stood, one hand on his cane, the other around the shoulder of his perfidious mistress as he surveyed the mistbound spectacle as if it were a vision of the apocalypse.

'What a romantic place for a last glimpse of your beloved England,' he sneered at Rosemary Fenton.

Crouch, snivelling and itching to shove her over the precipice, awaited his master's orders like a trained dog.

'Remove ze gag!' snapped Lenya von Brunno. 'I want to hear her scream.' She flourished her whip menacingly, but Crouch needed no further encouragement. Licking his lips, he dragged Rosemary to the ground.

'I won't scweam!' she shouted defiantly. 'I want to die!'

'How charming,' Lenya purred. 'Why?'

Rosemary took a deep breath. 'Because ... I'm ... no longer a ... virgin.' The disgrace, the humiliation of this fallen woman was evident and absolute. 'You *beast*, von Bwunno.'

The Count looked away guiltily.

'No longer a *virgin*?' Lenya repeated in a voice that would have cut through several layers of concrete. Then she modulated her tone to one of deep sympathy. 'What happened.'

Rosemary fought back the tears. 'He ... *touched* me ... in the rear seat...'

'So!' Lenya hissed accusingly.

'It was a matter of necessity,' protested the Count. 'Ze formula vas hidden in her underthings.'

'And no doubt you had to search *every* part of her body,' Lenya echoed with bitter sarcasm.

'It was an odious task—'

'That stretched your capacity to resist beyond its *breaking point*,' the Countess snarled, lashing at von Brunno with her whip and dislodging his monocle.

'We shall discuss this later!' roared the Count. Lenya glared at him with murder in her eyes, but kept silent. 'Crouch!' he snapped. 'Kill her!'

'Oh no! Help!' screamed Rosemary in terror, for Crouch was hooking his filthy white gloved hands underneath her arms, thus enabling him to massage her bosom for the last time as he dragged her towards the cliff-edge.

'Unfortunate that ze dashing Captain Crummond is dead and cannot rescue you,' snarled Lenya as Crouch, salivating, slumped Rosemary's exhausted body on the very knife edge of the steep precipice and prepared himself for the final push that would banish her for all time to the quarry's beckoning, black and brooding bottom...

24

In Which the Hun Nation Is Taught the Meaning of Pluck and How to Bat by the Rules and the British Empire Is Caught Out for a Duck and Stumped in the Goolies

'NOT AS DEAD as you think, von Brunno!' came a familiar voice.

As one, the von Brunnos, Crouch and Miss Fenton whipped round in astonishment.

From behind the Mercedes dashed Captain Hugh Crummond, his countenance grim and determined, his Webley pointed erect and lethal in his steely grip.

'You said he vas eliminated,' hissed Lenya to her fellow in felony with an evil stare.

Count Otto von Brunno was shaken. 'He was paralysed,' he hissed back, 'with dynamite in his mouth. I thought of everything.'

'Not quite!' Bullshot replied, vaulting athletically with one hand over the barrier, Webley still aimed with deadly accuracy at the hearts of his adversaries.

'When you directed Dobbs to the room where I was paralysed, there was one small thing you hadn't accounted for.'

Slowly and suavely he walked towards them. 'That he would be wearing our regimental club tie – which is one hundred per cent silk! The static electricity in it temporarily neutralised the force field, giving me time to take advantage of the inflammable properties of the brandy—'

He joined the von Brunnos at the cliff edge and turned deftly to Lenya.

'—that *you* offered me earlier.'

Lenya turned away, caught out in her perfidy, under the ferocious scowl of her joint-shareholder in the bonds of evil.

'Within the small amount of neck movement available to me under the magnetic paralysis, I formed my nasal cavity into a type of Liebig condenser – thereby concentrating the alcohol fumes in one place.'

He pinched his nose to demonstrate.

'I then forced the fumes down each nostril with such intensity that they combusted the lighted end of the dynamite, thus forming a natural blow torch—'

He pulled out the dynamite stick and blew it.

'—which completely severed the fuse, rendering the dynamite—'

He tossed the stick up in the air and caught it.

'—totally harmless.'

He replaced the dynamite stick in his inside pocket.

'The rest was easy.'

'Oh, Bullshot!' Rosemary sighed, her eyes swimming in admiration.

'And now you two blighters will be spending the rest of your lives in one of His Majesty's Prisons,' Crummond concluded.

It was game, set and match. The case of the theft of Professor Fenton's formula was closed. It only remained to tie up the loose ends, release the Professor, and place this pair of villains and their disreputable-looking lackey in the capable hands of the law.

Then it would be home to Mayfair for muffins and cocoa – and a brandy for Miss Fenton. She looked as though she could do with something big, strong and wet to pull her through the night. And he could do with one himself.

But the perfidious Countess made one last-ditch attempt to save her skin.

'Captain!' she purred seductively, couldn't you at least spare *me*? Remember yesterday? Ze fire! Ze passion!'

The Count turned in fury on Lenya, his eyes livid with jealousy. 'Ze brandy!' he added sardonically.

'Just ze two of us ... alone,' she sighed languidly.

Rosemary turned in fury to Bullshot. 'Hugh Crummond!' she squeaked. 'How could you?'

'She was masquerading as a war widow,' he protested, turning to her beseechingly.

For a split second he had taken his eyes off the Count, but it gave the Hun time enough to kick the pistol from his hand. It sailed over the cliff, gone forever. The cowardly Count, no longer fearful for his life, dealt Bullshot a despicable punch in the chin, which sent the Englishman reeling to the edge of the precipice.

But Hugh Crummond was not finished yet. 'So it's fisticuffs you want, von Brunno,' he exclaimed haughtily, climbing to his feet and starting to remove his jacket. 'In that case, I'm your man—'

The German cared nothing for sportsmanship or fair play. Not even allowing Crummond to manoeuvre himself into position, let alone finish removing his jacket, the dastardly ruffian kicked him in the shin. The Captain howled with pain, hopping backwards as he nursed the injured leg and then fell over a rock.

But two could play at that game. 'So you want to fight dirty?' he cried, climbing to his knees. 'One should expect that from a nation that never learned the rules of cricket – ooooohh!'

Taking advantage of a man when he was down was bad enough, but the brute had just kicked him in an unmentionable area.

'Why you bloody rapscallion!' Bullshot screeched in a high falsetto, charging at von Brunno, who had his back to the cliff edge. The German flipped him over in a crudely sneaky movement. But Bullshot's stamina was inexhaustible. He got to his feet again, now teetering on the very brink of the cliff, arms flailing in a desperate attempt to keep his balance.

With a careless nudge, the Black Baron of Blitzburg prodded Captain Crummond with his cane, tipping him over the edge.

Crummond let out a desperate howl as he disappeared into the canyon. Rosemary screamed and averted her eyes, but Otto and Lenya von Brunno only laughed uproariously.

'How quickly ze table turns!' sneered the Count, flourishing his cane. 'So, finally ze end of Bullshot Crummond!'

25

'NOT QUITE!' came a familiar voice.

As one, the von Brunnos, Crouch and Miss Fenton whipped round in astonishment.

Above the edge of the precipice peeked the eyes of Captain Hugh Crummond, looking grim and determined, his nose pointed erect and lethal in his steely head.

'There was one small thing you hadn't accounted for,' he said tersely, 'my training with the British Mountaineering Team across the Andes in 1924.'

'Twenty-four was ze year I won my Gold Medal for fencing,' sallied Count Otto von Brunno, unsheathing a rapier from his swordstick cane and holding the point to Bullshot's chin.

'Cut his throat, Otto!' Lenya urged viciously.

'No,' replied the Count. 'His death would be too quick. I have something much slower and more lingering in mind.'

He laughed at the back of his throat like a hound out of hell.

Hugh Crummond had been in some sticky situations in the course of his distinguished career. He thought back to the little affair of the Arabian Lunatic whom he had finally tracked down to a back street in Bangkok, only to find himself chained and gagged and imprisoned in a rat-filled sewer into which deadly nerve-gas had been pumped for three weeks. But compared with his present predicament, that had been like a day's grouse shooting on the moors with crumpets for tea.

He turned the upper part of his trunk as best he could to see how Rosemary was shaping up. She smiled back at him bravely. He had to admit it: she might only be a woman but she certainly had spunk.

They were standing in a sunken trough in the hellish dungeon of Netherington Manor, inside egg-shaped moulds, into which Crouch was shovelling a concrete-like mixture, whose evil-smelling fumes were forcing him to retch with nausea.

The concrete had already set around their legs and soon they would be fixed rigid in the mould, when it came up to their waists. What the fiendish Count intended to do with them then was anybody's guess, but it looked as though they would soon be in this thing right up to their necks.

'Happy, *Liebling?*' chanted Countess Lenya von Brunno. Drenched in high-collared fur, studded with dazzling rhinestones, as if stepping out for an evening at the opera, she linked arms with the Count as they descended the steps to a halfway landing stage from whose balcony they could observe Crouch at his odious handwork.

'Of course—' he replied '—and yet, this is tinged with regret … regret that I will never again draw my sabre against such a magnificent adversary.' He stamped his feet in a mocking salute.

'Spare me the compliments, von Brunno,' Bullshot replied wearily.

'I believe it is customary in these circumstances to grant one last request?' The Count oozed smarmy magnanimity.

'All right. Tell me this plan of yours to rule the world.'

'Why not, Otto?' said Lenya. 'He can take our secret to the grave.'

'Very well...' acceded the Count. 'Imagine a future where all ze oil supplies are controlled by ze Middle East.'

'*What?*' Crummond winced, horrified at the idea. 'My destiny in the hands of Bedouin Camel Drivers who eat sheep's eyes for breakfast? Poppycock!'

The Count held up his finger. 'Unless someone possesses a formula for synthetic fuel ... I...' He paused dramatically. '... am now that person!'

'So that's it!' Bullshot exclaimed to Rosemary.

'Daddy's formula was for synthetic fuel!' she exclaimed back.

'Precisely!' said the Count with a grin. 'And with it, I shall control an entire planet.'

Crummond snorted. 'If you're telling me that in years to come the world's economy will depend on oil, you're talking through your hat.'

He paused and his eyes took on a faraway look – the look of an Englishman who cherished an ideal and was prepared to fight for it.

'My vision of the future is far more practical. Massive global warfare. That will stimulate the economy, increase productivity and get the malingerers—'

He pointed disgustedly at Crouch, who had finished his job and, shovel against shoulder, was shuffling off to drink himself into a stupor.

'—out of the unemployment lines and back into the trenches where they belong.'

'Bwavo, Hugh!' cried Rosemary, clapping enthusiastically. 'At least it will give them a cause and a cup of warm soup.'

The Count stared at the English couple, imprisoned and fixed in their moulds, with disbelief. 'They are more dangerous lunatics than even I had believed,' he said to Lenya. 'Their demise will not come a moment too soon.'

He departed, but Lenya lingered for a moment, loathe to tear her eyes away from Hugh Crummond for the last time.

'*Auf wiedersehen*, Captain,' she said huskily. 'What a pity so many things were left undone.'

'Like your skirt, for instance,' Bullshot called out contemptuously. 'You Hun she-devil.'

She laughed throatily as she disappeared up the steps, but Rosemary did not see the joke.'

'How could you?' she screamed angrily at Crummond.

'That's how I saw the tattoo on her thigh,' he tried to reason with her.

'Hugh Cwummond,' she yelled. 'I never want to speak to you again as long as I live!'

He looked down at the fast-setting concrete that now pinioned them up to the waist in their respective moulds. Suddenly water gushed out of a pipe above their heads and they began to rock and swivel as the moulds were dashed this way and that. Rosemary shrieked.

'Judging by the force of the water, that won't be much longer,' he said grimly. 'If we assume that the Starkey and Murchison outlet valve has a standard thrust pressure of eighty pounds per square inch, and the capacity in here is ... 22,240 cubic centimetres ... well, you can figure it out for yourself.'

Rosemary was completely baffled.

'We've got about twenty-four and a half minutes,' he summed up.

'Don't change the subject!' cried Rosemary, her frustration intensified because for once she was quite unable to stamp her foot. 'Your behaviour with that von Bwunno woman was *unspeakable!*'

'By Jove,' Bullshot replied, 'you're beautiful when you're angry!'

Romantically he leaned towards her, rolling his egg-shaped mould until it almost tipped over, but Rosemary leaned back to avoid him. Soon they were rocking back and forth like rubber ducks in a bath, arms flailing wildly to keep their balance, which only increased the momentum of the rocking, rolling mounds. Suddenly their heads banged together and they both winced in pain.

'Get away from me, Hugh Cwummond!' Rosemary yelled indignantly as the water bubbled around her. 'There are plenty of other fish in the sea.'

Through a grille in the room above, Professor Fenton

gazed with shock and horror as the water lapped around the English couple.

'What kind of people are you,' he shouted indignantly at the laughing Count, 'who can drown innocent people in concrete egg-cups?'

26

IN WHICH SOMETHING SOFT, WET AND SQUIDGY
MOVES UNDER MISS FENTON'S LEGS
AND STARTS UP CAPTAIN CRUMMOND'S
FEROCIOUS LAGONDA

ORD BINKY BRANCASTER sat reluctantly at the wheel of his old chum Bullshot's open tourer. Dressed in his leather coat and goggles, he revved up the engine.

'That's it, your Lordship, easy does it,' called out Dobbs from the driveway of Crummond's country estate. 'Now just a bit more choke.'

'Do I really have to substitute for old Crummond?' Binky complained. 'I'm so dreadful with mechanical things.'

Dobbs shook his head. 'He was most insistent, your Lordship. He's won six years in a row, you know. Some people are starting to call it the Crummond Cup.'

Binky's face was a picture of misery. 'Couldn't you at least navigate for me, Dobbs? A chap might easily lose his bally way!'

'No, sorry sir, can't,' Dobbs replied unmoved. 'Captain's on a case, sir. And he left strict instructions that if he hadn't telephoned me here by ten o'clock, I was to get in touch with Scotland Yard.'

As Binky lurched off erratically round the circular driveway and into the road going south. Dobbs gave him an encouraging thumbs-up sign, shaking his head sceptically.

The church clock was striking ten as he reached the house.

Two heads and necks bobbed in a sea of water, as the gushing continued.

'Oh, Hugh...' sighed Rosemary, close to despair.

Crummond had to admit that things looked pretty grim.

'I'm afraid time's running out, Rosemary,' he said stoically. 'Two minutes for me. Two minutes and twenty-three seconds for you.'

'Why longer for me?' she asked.

'You're wearing high heels.'

Rosemary felt somehow so close to Hugh at this moment. 'I'm sorry I was so beastly to you,' she sighed. 'Let's be fwiends.'

'I'd hoped we would be more than that, Rosemary,' he replied seriously. 'I had a dream ... a modest little house, somewhere in the Cotswolds. The two of us exercising spaniels as the sun set over the apple orchards. Lazy summer days ... you planning menus with Cook while I'm gassing badgers ... in the meadow.'

It was as if a new day had dawned.

'You mean there was nothing between you and that ghastly Lenya von Bwunno?'

'Of course not,' Bullshot replied with passionate intensity. 'You know I only have eyes for you.'

Somewhere far off, birds sang and church bells rang.

'Me too, Hugh,' sighed Rosemary all aglow, and wet. 'It was you, Hugh – only ever you, Hugh.'

'At least we can share heaven together,' he said, gazing deep into her eyes.

'What will heaven be like?' she asked. She was a little girl once more, sitting at her father's knee.

'England,' Crummond declared at once, and from the very core of his being, 'on a June afternoon!'

'Church bells in the distance?'

He nodded.

'Stwawbewwies and cweam for tea?'

He nodded. '*And we'll be thrashing Australia at cricket!*' he added with heartfelt conviction.

'Oh!' Rosemary sighed. '*Oh!*' she gurgled the next moment as water began to lap around her chin. 'Goodbye, darling Hugh...'

'Blub-bye, Blosebary...' he gurgled from beneath the surface.

The water level moved inexorably towards Bullshot's nostrils.

'*Oh!*' Rosemary suddenly screamed. '*The concwete's gone all squidgy! Oh, Hugh!*'

'Bwbwbwbw,' Crummond gurgled back. 'You're right! And I've managed to work my leg loose!' he yelled. 'Hold on, Rosemary!'

The three-time Olympic Gold Medal swimming champion crashed through the water, his powerful crawl stroke making easy meat of the distance between them.

'They're breaking free!' exclaimed Lenya von Brunno, peering through the grille of the observation room.

The dim, dark-shadowed eyes of Professor Fenton lit up. 'Ha!' he exclaimed. 'More infamous villains than you have tried to get rid of Bullshot Crummond, and failed!'

The Count looked venomous.

'Ah, Otto, please let me eliminate him,' Lenya implored, silkily stroking his bald pate.

'No!' he cried, the worm of a fiendish idea already burrowing its way through his craggy skull. 'I think ze gallant Captain deserves … *Myra!*'

He pulled a lever on the control panel. The sluice gate opened.

Beyond it, something started to move…

27

In Which Captain Crummond Wrestles with Eight Talking Tentacles and Goes Down for the Count

With Rosemary squirming and struggling on top of him, Crummond swam to the side of the pool.

'The water's stopping!' she screamed excitedly. 'We're safe!'

'I'm not so sure,' he declared. The sluice gate had been raised and he had just spotted an ominous movement beyond it. 'Quick!' he ordered, and swam with her to the far side of the pool.

'Here! There's a ledge!' he shouted, holding his hands in a stirrup position to give a bunk-up. 'Now give me your hand.'

With a certain amount of difficulty and much wobbling, Rosemary stepped up and negotiated herself on the ledge; Bullshot jumped up after her.

'No!' he snapped. 'We must make our way to that doorway over there. Excuse me.'

The ledge was very narrow and, crossing in front of her, Crummond was forced to press his body hard against hers. Rosemary's eyes seemed to widen and go a little goggly as he jiggled up and down in his progress past her.

'There,' he said as he reached the other side.

For a moment Rosemary was too carried away to speak, but suddenly she screamed again as the huge tentacle of a gigantic octopus wrapped itself around Bullshot's waist and pulled him howling back into the water up to his thighs. Then another tentacle thrust itself between his legs and tried to grab her leg.

'*Aaaagh! Aaaagh! Aaaagh!*' she screamed. '*Stop it, Hugh!*'

The tentacle around Bullshot's waist was yanking him up and down, sending strange vibrations through his body.

'Aaagh! I can't control this thing between my legs!' he shouted. 'It's got a mind of its own! Grab it!'

The huge extended tentacle moved up beneath Rosemary's dress and grabbed her leg.

'It's so shiny and wubbery!' piped Rosemary, then her eyes seemed to glaze over and she added in a deep, throaty voice, 'And it's *so big!*'

'Grab it, Rosemary!' he shouted back. 'Grab it!'

'I can't!' she squeaked. 'We're not married!'

'Forget about marriage' Hugh screamed frantically. 'Beat it off! Beat it off!'

The tentacle was wrapping itself around her neck and with a sudden lashing movement it dragged her screaming into the water.

'As you see, Professor, I am ze fortunate possessor of ze only trained octopus in ze world,' von Brunno boasted as Myra continued to thrash about madly, dragging the couple capriciously in, out and across the water. 'Observe: *Myra! Bala Mafu Kana. Calamara-wa.*'

He spoke the octopus-ese through an ornate tube in the control panel.

'Oh no, not that!' exclaimed Professor Fenton in horror as the von Brunnos laughed darkly at the disgusting instruction. 'Spare my daughter and I'll work for you for the rest of my life.'

'We don't need you any more, Professor, now that we have your formula,' said Lenya, brushing past him and turned her head to deliver a cold, lethal smile to his petrified eyes.

'I have other inventions,' said the Professor hastily. 'Weapons of awesome destruction.'

'Awesome destruction?' repeated the Count, turning away from the grille. 'Tell me more.'

'Release my daughter first,' demanded the Professor.

'Very well,' replied von Brunno and spoke into the tube. '*Myra! Malla! Malla! Rosemary Fenton Carbeessa pr Kong!* Crouch!' he added through another tube. 'Release ze Fenton girl.'

Rosemary screamed as the tentacles lashed around her mercilessly through the water, but on the Count's command they suddenly went slack. She sighed with relief, but then noticed Crouch staggering down the steps to rescue her – and screamed even louder.

Crouch was more tenacious than the octopus, however, and soon had his tentacles locked around her bosom once more. He dragged her out of the cellar, her screams slowly becoming fainter as she slumped unconscious at last in his slimy arms.

But Bullshot's battle with Myra was reaching its terrible climax. For a few seconds he seemed to have the upper hand, but three of Myra's tentacles suddenly dragged him under. Gradually the surface of the water returned to mirror stillness.

All at once a tentacle shot out of the water in a victorious Excalibur gesture.

Of Captain Hugh Crummond there was no trace.

28

IN WHICH DOBBS INSTRUCTS HIS MASTER'S FRIEND TO THROTTLE A MOTORCAR AND LENYA DESTRUCTS HIS MASTER'S VOICE TO THROTTLE MISS FENTON

'A TOAST, LENYA. The promise I made to you all those years ago has finally been kept.'

Count Otto von Brunno linked arms with Lenya's as they raised their champagne glasses.

'I owe you everything, *Liebchen*,' she sighed. 'Imagine! I was once an obscure cabaret singer, and soon I will stand beside you as Mistress of ze World!'

They drank and smashed their glasses against the fireplace.

'Prepare to leave,' announced the Count. 'Tonight we dine in our beloved Berlin.'

Lenya kissed his wrist and swept out; the Count turned to Professor Fenton, who once more was tied securely into a chair.

'Professor,' he barked, leaning over the chair and peering down at him. 'You will continue your work here, under Crouch's supervision.'

This was the final indignity. 'I gave my word as an Englishman,' he replied testily. 'Isn't that enough?'

'Of course,' the Count sneered, 'but if you fail to co-operate, Crouch will know what to do to your daughter…'

The Professor scowled furiously, but then a thought

struck him. 'This chap Crouch,' he asked matter-of-factly. 'Married, is he?'

Across the English countryside careered the police car, its bell ringing madly as it roared through a sleepy village. Inside the car sat two uniformed policemen, one plain-clothes policeman and one well-uniformed ex-batman. Without slowing down or signalling, it swung into the opposite lane, overtaking a rally car.

Lord Binky Brancaster panicked and swerved on the grass verge as Dobbs leaned out of the window of the passing police car and called, 'More throttle, your Lordship!'

Looking thoroughly fed up, Binky somehow managed to get back on the road and wave a feeble thank you to the rapidly disappearing police car.

Rosemary Fenton was still lying unconscious on the bed as Lenya von Brunno entered her bedroom. The Englishwoman stirred sleepily and opened her eyes to observe the German revealing her disgraceful black-lace underwear as she slipped out of her dress.

With beating heart, the recent encounter with the octopus returned to her and with it the terrible memory of Crouch's filthy hands and of sweet, wonderful Hugh disappearing beneath the murky water.

But there was no time to be lost. Daddy's life could

still be in danger and the world still needed saving from the wicked designs of these beastly madmen.

Suddenly she noticed the aviator's outfit on a hanger that Lenya had taken from the wardrobe and the seeds of an idea began to form. Just in time she closed her eyes as the Countess turned to look at her contemptuously.

'I ought to kill you,' she hissed. 'You are ze voman he zought of vhen I vas in his arms.'

This was too much for Rosemary. She sprang to life, and lunged at Lenya. In seconds, they were fighting like vicious cats, tearing at each other's hair and ripping at each other's clothes. To her mortification Rosemary's dress was soon in shreds, her peach satin cami-knickers exposed to the sneering eyes of her opponent.

From the fireplace Lenya grabbed a poker and advanced on Rosemary, who screamed and snapped off one of the curved posts from the four-poster bed. With these lethal weapons they embarked on an impromptu, home-made sword fight: Lenya moving as stealthily as a predatory tiger, Rosemary more like a flustered ostrich or a prancing circus horse as she ran awkwardly about the room, screaming hysterically, knees almost touching her chin.

Rosemary clambered up a sideboard and clutched the curtain rail above the window, but Lenya was ahead of her: she pulled the cords on the opposite side of the window and swung Rosemary back towards her. Rosemary then jumped on the bed, which bounced like a trampoline and as Lenya tried to lash her with her whip, spitting oaths at her in German, Rosemary only just managed to avoid being lacerated by jumping up and down until she had built up enough height to vault across the room. In her turn, she advanced on Lenya and skewered her earring viciously to the wall with a hatpin.

Lenya countered this by ripping out the huge brass horn from the gramophone. She swung it wildly around her, laughing like a maniac as she forced Rosemary backwards onto the bed and prepared to plunge it over the Englishwoman's head.

29

In Which Science is Unchained from an Armchair and Sorcery is Unplugged from a Four-Poster Bed

'HA! WHO IS THAT?' exclaimed the Professor, still cocooned in the cat's cradle that bound him to the chair, as he heard a noise behind him.

But Hugh Crummond was a man in a hurry and had no time for idle chit-chat or time-wasting explanations as he rushed into the main hall and confronted the Professor.

'Crummond, you're alive!' shouted the boffin with hoarse excitement.

Looking immaculate as ever, Bullshot began unlassoing the ropes.

'I thought that dreadful octopus had disposed of you,' exclaimed Professor Fenton in wonder and admiration. 'How on earth did you manage to escape her clutches?'

Only now did Hugh Crummond pause, and smile. 'There was one small thing the von Brunnos hadn't accounted for,' he replied with an air of mystery. 'My knowledge of undersea languages. Within the small amount of neck movement available to me between the octopus's tentacles, I rearranged my voice-box to approximate that of a giant killer whale – Myra's natural predator.'

'Good Lord!' the Professor exclaimed, looking at the

man with new eyes. 'You must have forced it into a rhomboid oblong.'

'Precisely, Professor!' replied Crummond.

Fired with enthusiasm he began to pace about the hall, leaving the Professor still strapped to his harness. 'Leaving only the problem of diaphragmatic thrust.'

The Professor considered this for a few seconds. Then he said excitedly, 'That means you must have inverted the water pressure on your larynx!'

'Only a man of science would appreciate that,' Hugh replied, pleased as punch. 'I then vibrated my lower dorsal cavity and forced the small amount of air I had left in it through my nose.' He put his hand to his chest and made a strange sound rather like the expulsion of wind: "*Mulla Baffa Ging Wha!*" Which is, of course, octopus-ese for "Me King of Undersea Beasts—".'

'"All in my way, die!"' the Professor completed, looking delightedly at this really remarkable mortal.

For a moment the decrepit, exhausted old man and the athletic, resourceful young man – one strapped to his chair, the other free as the wind – were united in a common bond, two original, penetrating minds leaping the barriers of age, physical prowess and function in a pure, altruistic quest to prise out the secrets of nature, explore the workings of the universe for the benefit of mankind and the greater glory of the Empire.

Bullshot sighed. 'Myra quivered like a jelly fish,' he finished, 'and the rest was easy.'

'Splendid, Crummond,' spluttered the Professor excitedly. 'You ought to write a paper on this.'

'You shall have it first thing in the morning, sir,' Bullshot smiled. Suddenly he grew serious. 'But where's Rosemary?'

The Professor looked disappointed. 'Oh, von

Brunno's doing something to her upstairs,' he replied in a tone of utter boredom and disinterest, waving his one free leg vaguely.

'*What!*' Bullshot exploded, and stormed off up the stairs.

The elderly boffin felt a little peeved: he had been hoping to engage this extraordinary young man in a dialogue about the chemical synthesis of human brain cells employing his latest discovery – silicon wafers, aluminium foil, vaporised sugar and candle wax. He had not yet worked out the ramifications or applications, but he was very much looking forward to experimenting on Crouch. A judicious piece of brain surgery could well make a definite improvement…

With a sigh, he rose stiffly.

Meanwhile Bullshot had crashed into the bedroom.

'*Rosemary!*' he cried, then stopped abruptly as his eyes fell on the terrible vision before him on the four-poster bed. He grimaced with disgust and nausea.

A female form, dressed only in black lace underwear, lay sprawled wantonly on white ermine; the huge brass gramophone horn that completely hooded her head was bobbing up and down in a slow, evil rhythm, as she breathed and moaned deeply and huskily.

'Rosemary!' His voice was now mixed with shock, regret and resignation. 'Oh, no, too late. Von Brunno has taken advantage of you.' He stood with his arms stiffly by his side and considered the sacrifice he had been about to make. 'And I would have married you!'

'Married!' came an excited voice from behind him.

Bullshot turned as the Professor, his limbs creaking as though he were a clockwork toy after their long captivity, arrived in time to witness the distasteful scene.

'I had hoped to, sir, but, under the circumstances…'

'Yes, quite out of the question, old boy,' sighed the Professor, his hopes of discharging his paternal responsibility once again foiled as he scientifically calculated that Rosemary's prospects of eligibility were now below zero, measured on the barometer of human decency.

He placed an avuncular arm around Crummond's shoulder as they turned their backs on the embarrassment. 'Now what am I going to do with the girl?' he grumbled in despair.

'May I suggest a nursing assignment in some remote corner of the Empire?' said Bullshot, man to man.

The Professor looked interested. 'I have a sister-in-law who works with pygmies in Tanganyika,' he mused.

This intriguing line of thought was interrupted by a lustful moan. A bejewelled hand reached up, curled around Crummond's neck and pinned him on his back to the bed.

Lenya von Brunno – for it was indeed she – having removed the huge brass hood, had sprung back on Bullshot like a black widow spider preparing to mate again with her male prey before finally devouring him.

Naked, but for the flimsy underwear, and arching her lithe, supple back as she leant over Bullshot longingly, she sighed with undisguised carnal pleasure.

'Captain, you came back! Take me!' She coiled herself over him and kissed him passionately.

'Yeeeuuccchhhh!' vomited Crummond in disgust as he freed himself from her embrace and wiped the scarlet lipstick from his sullied mouth. 'You *vixen!*'

'Where is my daughter?' asked the Professor as, with a mixture of anxiety and relief, he turned up the white ermine coverlet on Lenya's bed, hoping a little, yet fearing more, to find her in some drugged and disgraceful condition between Lenya's sheets.

'If you don't tell us,' Bullshot snapped, pointing his finger at her menacingly, 'it's curtains for you!'

'I think not,' replied Lenya disdainfully. 'Look behind you, Captain Crummond!'

As she spoke, Crouch staggered and slouched into the bedroom, a Luger in his loathsome, foetid fist.

'Oh no, I don't fall for that old trick,' Crummond replied with weary scepticism, not bothering to look round.

The terrified Professor was patting him urgently on the shoulder. At last Bullshot turned, and instantly raised his hands.

'Crouch!' barked the Countess. 'Kill him!'

Crouch raised his gun and pointed it at Crummond's heart – but something seemed to sir in his little piggy eyes and he hesitated.

'Now!' ordered Lenya, losing patience.

For a second Crouch seemed to curdle in a state of indecision. Then something awful happened.

Crouch spoke.

30

IN WHICH A GANGLING GOGGLY-EYED GIGGLER GAMBOLS IN HER GOGGLES AND A GRUNTING GURGLING GARGOYLE GAMBLES ON HIS GUNNERY

CROUCH'S COCKROACH EYES crawled over the Countess.

'I couldn't do that, Miss,' he growled, the vocal cords rusted and rotten after years of silence. 'Captain Crummond, the gun's for you!'

'What!' Bullshot was thunderstruck as Crouch handed him the Luger. 'I don't understand.'

Crouch moved nearer to him, grinning horrible bonhomie, breath like sewage.

'You don't recognise me, do you, sir?' he croaked.

Crummond backed away from him distastefully. 'Can't say that I do,' he admitted.

Crouch snuffled. 'We fought together in the Loamshires.'

Bullshot peered dubiously at this walking disease. 'Good grief!' he exploded, firing on all cylinders. 'Surely you're not Stanley "Lofty" Crouch, my old bombardier!'

Crouch looked abashed. 'The same, sir,' he grunted, saluting.

'But Lofty was a handsome six foot four,' Crummond protested.

'I know, sir,' confessed the stunted lackey, 'but after you misread my hand signals and ran over me in that tank you was learning to drive, I lost a few inches.' He sighed and Bullshot was again forced to retreat from the stench.

'The experience made me bitter and I became a bad'un. That's why I joined up with this lot.'

Lenya, hands poised like twin spiders, bared her teeth and darted a look of pure venom at the turncoat.

Crummond's mind was racing. 'Wait!' he exclaimed, pointing the stem of his pipe at Crouch. 'The concrete blocks!'

'Right, sir,' admitted Crouch smugly. 'I had a change of heart. Instead of cement I used Miss Fenton's scone recipe. I gambled that the water would make them soggy.'

'Good Lord!' piped up the Professor in astonishment. 'Nothing else ever did!'

'Treacherous swine,' hissed Lenya lunging at the renegade.

But Bullshot was too fast for her: he seized her wrist in a ferocious Indian-wrestle grip and forced her backwards. Defeated, she arched her voluptuous semi-naked form against the four-poster bed, strangely stirred by the strength of this tenacious, inexhaustible man. What a pity he didn't worship evil as she did.

Hugh Crummond was like a fireball. 'Professor!' he ordered. 'Keep both eyes on this she-devil.'

'My pleasure, Captain,' replied Fenton, who had not felt so alive in years.

'Now where's von Brunno?' Bullshot demanded with crisp authority.

'Escaping in his secret plane, sir,' replied Crouch snappily, once more a bombardier, a human being, but above all, one of the team. Captain Crummond had truly achieved a miracle.

'With Rosemary?' asked Crummond in alarm.

'But I sabotaged the synthetic fuel!' exclaimed the Professor. 'That plane will never make it across the English Channel!'

'*What!*' Bullshot thundered, rushing for the door, followed by Crouch – no longer slouching but sprinting like a demon – leaving Lenya von Brunno to the care of Professor Fenton, and vice versa. For the scheming seductress was not yet done.

Eyes blazing, she lifted her black-stockinged leg and slid it provocatively along the erect upright support of the four-poster bed, staring challengingly at the Professor as the aged boffin backed away in alarm.

The little red-painted De Havilland Fox Moth passenger plane taxied towards its take-off position along the long grass of a field sheltered from the prying eyes of the world by tall, shady trees.

A willowy figure dressed in a flying suit climbed awkwardly over a stile and ran towards it in a curious ducklike motion, knees almost touching chin. The wide anxious eyes of Rosemary Fenton were for a moment visible before she donned her goggles and climbed into the cabin – forward of the cockpit – and closed the door.

Inside the cockpit, Count Otto von Brunno sat impatiently waiting for her to strap herself into her passenger seat.

'Lenya!' he called out through the circular aperture that connected the cockpit with the cabin in front of him. 'Thanks to ze Professor's formula, we will be able to reach ze Fatherland without refuelling!'

Rosemary pulled up the collar of her flying suit to hide her apprehensive face as the Black Baron of Blitzburg taxied the plane forward.

'Prepare for take-off!' he shouted ominously.

As the De Havilland was grazing the edge of the grass, a police car was approaching the field along a country lane. And as the car screeched to a halt by a gate at the entrance to the field, Hugh Crummond was racing down the lane behind it.

'Out of my way!' he yelled as Dobbs and the policemen climbed out of the car. 'The gal I love is on that plane!'

He scrambled past them and, with the grace and speed of a panther, vaulted over the high gate and tore through the field, frantically chasing the plane as it began to leave the ground two hundred yards ahead of him.

'He'll never make it!' shouted the plain-clothes policeman watching from the gate.

For once it seemed that Captain Crummond was running an unwinnable race. For the plane was steadily gaining height as it lifted its nose victoriously in a south-easterly direction towards Germany and soared away from the Sussex countryside, carrying with it Miss Rosemary Fenton and a formula that would hold the entire planet under the power of its evil pilot, who laughed satanically as he pulled on his joystick and said goodbye to England.

31

In Which the Captain Has a Plane to Catch and the Professor Has a Shoulder to Cry On

'I WOULDN'T BET on it, sir,' said Dobbs confidently to the sceptical detective. 'I reckon the Captain will break his own world record from the Amsterdam Olympics.'

The De Havilland was gaining altitude every second and, as Bullshot hurled himself across the grass, its speed was definitely increasing. But such was the ferocity of Hugh Crummond's sprint that the gap between his nose and the tailplane was decreasing second by second.

His legs, though not long, had the natural – some have said unnatural or even supernatural – muscle-to-weight ratio of a greyhound and it seemed to Dobbs and the Scotland Yard officer who witnessed this awesome spectacle that he was not running *through* the grass but *on* it or even *above* it.

For what Dobbs had omitted to mention to the policeman was that Hugh Crummond held three unbroken Olympic and World records, for the hundred yard sprint, the long jump and the high jump. He was now in top gear, accelerating like a finely tuned racing car and as the plane arose fifteen feet above him, he concentrated all his energy into one mad leap.

For a moment he seemed to soar into the sky like an eagle, his arms stretched diagonally above him with nothing but his own momentum to carry him forward. His hands reached out but there was only the wind to clutch and it seemed that once again the Black Baron of Blitzburg had bested him.

But suddenly his fingers made magical contact with the biplane's undercarriage and, with a strength fuelled by a clear conscience, a moderate diet, temperance in his drinking habits and a clean-living abstinence from practices that would sap the energies of lesser mortals, together with sheer will power and the necessary muscular control gained by his final year in the Public School Welter Weights, he clung to the crossbeams, swinging from the plane like a trapeze artist as it soared into the clouds.

'Is there no limit to that man's tenacity?' said the detective in awe.

Dobbs smiled to himself. 'I'd better get back to London,' he replied, turning back to the car. 'The Captain will be wanting a hot bath when all this is over.'

Like a spider dangling from its web, Captain Crummond hung upside down from the De Havilland's under-carriage, his feet trying to make purchase with the wing, as inside the plane Count Otto von Brunno schemed and gloated and glanced out of the cockpit to sneer at the green and fair patchwork quilt of countryside that was England.

'Lenya!' he called out to his passenger. 'Take a last look at England, that insignificant *rock* off ze German coast!'

For the first time since boarding the plane, Rosemary spoke.

'Otto,' she called, affecting Lenya's accent, 'are you weally sure you have ze formula safe?'

'Yes, right here,' snapped the Count irritably.

'Why not let *me* look after it?' she suggested, holding her breath as the Count hesitated.

'Very well,' he called out at last, and handed it to her through the aperture between the cabin and the cockpit.

Stifling her nervous excitement, Rosemary pocketed it.

Meanwhile Captain Crummond, with the skill and daring of an acrobat and the expertise of an ace fighter pilot, had landed on the wing and was beginning his slow, tortuous and delicately balanced progress towards the cockpit – when once again he would be face to face with his deadly foe.

And now, once again, Rosemary Fenton was to demonstrate that peculiarly English and somehow uniquely feminine pluck that had drawn him so magnetically towards her from the start. She thrust her arm through the aperture and grabbed the Count's joystick.

As Hugh Crummond had already discovered, the girl had spunk.

'What are you doing?' shouted von Brunno in alarm.

With a sudden lurch the plane swooped downwards, almost jolting Bullshot off the wing: he clung desperately to it as he lay fully outstretched on his stomach.

The plane continued to plummet earthwards.

'Lenya!' the Count screamed as he yanked Rosemary's arm loose and pulled back on the joystick. 'What are you trying to do – kill us both?'

'It's not Lenya,' Rosemary shouted in her own high-pitched voice as she poked through the aperture and triumphantly removed her goggles to reveal hew own goggly eyes. 'It's me – *Wosemawy Fenton!*'

'*Gott in Himmel!*' screamed the Count in fury. 'Give me back that formula!' He thrust his arm through the aperture and poked it about, but in vain.

'Never!' she cried with bold defiance, as she removed her helmet. 'You're beaten, von Bwunno! And the World is a safer place!'

And then Rosemary Fenton executed the most extraordinary act of heroism a mere woman has ever performed in the recorded history of the world. Opening the cabin door, she flung herself, and her father's formula, out of the plane to a certain death, thereby saving mankind from the dire consequences of the Black Baron of Blitzburg's plan to enslave the human race.

The fact that Rosemary's flying suit happened to incorporate a parachute could almost certainly be discounted as it was highly unlikely that any woman, and Rosemary Fenton in particular, would have the remotest idea how to deploy the ripcord in order to avoid hurtling towards oblivion.

The Count stared out of his cockpit with amazement and horror as his formula and Rosemary Fenton plummeted towards the English countryside.

But now the inglorious von Brunno had other problems with which to contend. An avenging angel called Bullshot Crummond stood before the Count on the opposite wing and paused dramatically, waiting for the Count to turn his head away from the staggering spectacle of the fallen Miss Fenton and her falling formula.

Growing impatient, Bullshot tapped him on the shoulder – and immediately pulled his hand back as though he had just touched a hot coal.

The Count jumped in astonishment and Crummond granted him one of his famous jaunty little nods.

Quickly von Brunno regained his composure. 'So, Captain,' he said cheerfully. 'It ends as it began! At five thousand feet. But this time you are without a plane!'

He gave the joystick a sharp tug and the De Havilland jerked, pushing Bullshot off-balance. He fell from the wing and once again found himself hanging desperately from the plane, this time clinging to the cockpit.

'I may have lost ze formula, Crummond, but at least I shall have ze satisfaction of seeing ze end of you,' the Count shouted, and viciously punched Hugh's faltering fingers until, one by one, they retired defeated and Bullshot parted company with the plane.

With an evil laugh and a farewell wave – an ancient Teutonic gesture – the Black Baron of Blitzburg flew on … and Captain Crummond flew down.

32
In Which You Will Truly Believe that an Englishman Can Fly

UGH CRUMMOND had been thrown out of some pretty nasty places in his time. He recalled the Caucasian Ectrodactyl who had tried to throttle him with his lobster claw hands as Bullshot hung from a precipice close to the summit of Mount Elbrus, thus causing him to plunge to what for any other mortal would have been certain death had he not reduced the velocity of his fall to that of a feather simply by visualising himself as a shuttlecock.

He remembered the Tree Man of Timbuktu who had chucked him two thousand feet down a poisoned well beneath a sand dune, when he had managed to escape being buried alive by using a meditative technique that enabled him to increase the water content in his body to nearly one hundred per cent. Then, with the aid of a form of levitation know only to a select number of Sufi initiates, he had literally transformed himself into a gushing fountain, which, when released from the well, was able to irrigate the surrounding area of the Sahara and thus bring life and hope to many thousands of grateful indigents.

Or there was the time when he had wrestled with the suicidal Eskimo Arsonist-Anarchist in the Arctic Circle to prevent him from blowing up the Earth's ice caps. Although Bullshot had eventually prevailed and saved the world from total destruction by global warming, in his dying moments the Eskimo had plunged him into a melting glacier, out of which he had only been able to steam his way by raising his body temperature to over two hundred degrees Fahrenheit.

But Bullshot had never before been thrown out of a plane without a parachute and, he had to admit to himself, this really took the biscuit. As the Earth toppled and spun towards him, his mind raced as he summoned up a lifetime's skill and experience, an encyclopaedic knowledge of every subject known to man and a million others known only to him.

And then he remembered a trick that had come in pretty handy when, Zulu-hunting out in Africa, he had been obliged to take refuge on the topmost branch of a mahogany tree from a vicious herd of five-toed climbing tree mice whose ferocious little bites would surely have put paid to his hopes of winning Gold in the major events of the Paris Olympics of 1924.

We should note here that even were Bullshot to have lost a limb or two, winning Silver or Bronze in every Olympic event would still have been on the cards for him – excepting, for obvious reasons, ladies' netball and lacrosse – although it goes without saying that anything less than Gold would have been a complete waste of his precious time.

But back to that mahogany tree. Within the small amount of neck movement available to him, Bullshot had rearranged his facial structure to resemble that of the African eagle, which is of course the five-toed tree mouse's natural predator. He had then vibrated his lower dorsal cavity, forcing the small amount of wind he had left into his lungs, and forming his arms into a bow shape that approximated that of the eagle's wings, thus enabling him by a series of oscillations to navigate himself to a clearing in the jungle where he happened to know the Zulu were pretty hot on the ground.

But this time it was going to be a little more tricky. There were very few Zulus living in the Sussex countryside that he could just about make out many furlongs beneath his falling feet. He quickly calculated his height and thrust, taking into account wind speeds, air pressures and temperatures, and of course humidity at lower levels, and set off in a north-north-westerly direction towards a conveniently placed parachute that was floating below him.

'Rosemary!' he called out, as he recognised the figure in the harness and, altering course by a strategic arm movement, he was soon speeding towards her.

'Oh, Hugh!' she gasped as he flew past her, but just in time he caught hold of her foot For several seconds he hung from it until he was in a position to climb upwards. Fortunately his mountaineering training came in useful as he moved hand over hand up Rosemary's legs until, reaching a natural fissure, he made it to base camp, inserting his head between the V of her thighs.

Rosemary's eyes seemed to widen and go a little gooey as he performed this operation and for a minute she was unable to speak, so hard was her concentration in accommodating Bullshot's head between her legs.

After a decent interval he renewed his attempt at the summit and was soon straddling her hips and waist and fought to gain a hold on her twin peaks. Rosemary helped with great enthusiasm, until at last he reached the plateau of her shoulders. With a sigh of contentment she cradled him in her arms as he sat in her lap and the parachute floated down like white blossom to earth.

'I knew you wouldn't let me down!' she sighed. 'And the pawachute came in handy too!'

'Top hole, Rosemary! Well done!' he shouted cheerfully and then paid her the highest compliment he could think of. 'Dash it, if you weren't a girl, you'd make a jolly fine chap!'

To prove it he gave her a smacker of a kiss on her chin.

Rosemary sighed with bliss and then gave a little squeal as he overbalanced. His arms lost hold of her and, with an urgent strength born of desperation, he clamped his legs around her hips, causing Rosemary to squeal even more. Finally he was able to push himself upright, knotting his arms around her neck as they sailed closer and closer to the ground.

'Hang on, Hugh!' she squeaked.

With an enormous bang they made it.

'How can I ever thank you for evewything you've

done?' she sighed.

'That would take far too long,' he had to concede. 'And we're not quite out of it yet.'

She looked down: they were now suspended from a railway signal on a road bridge beside a railway track and they were bobbing up and down as the elasticity of the parachute cord diminished second by second.

'According to my knowledge of Bradshaw's Railway Timetable, the 4.28 from Tunbridge Wells to Haywards Heath will be passing through here any minute. And when that signal drops our parachute cords will slip ortt...' As he spoke, an open car whizzed past beneath, a rally number fixed to its side.

'And we'll fall into the woad below,' cried Rosemary in panic. 'We'll both be killed.'

She began to scream.

33

In Which Bullshot and Rosemary Drop in on Binky for a Flying Visit

'NOT NECESSARILY,' said Hugh Crummond. Rosemary, panic about to turn to hysteria, stopped screaming and gazed at him, awaiting the oracle.

'If memory serves, this is the London-to-Brighton Road.'

He crushed her head against his shoulder as he consulted his watch.

'And it's four fifty-two and three-quarters. Now if Binky's up to par and the car's going like a rocket, he should be through at precisely four fifty—'

As the train approached, it blew its whistle warningly. The signal dropped. Rosemary felt the rush of air as they fell from the bridge.

'—three,' completed Crummond from the back of his own Lagonda into which, just as he had foreseen, they had been dropped with clinical precision.

'Good Lord, Crummond, what have you been up to?' asked Binky at the wheel, who, to be frank, was more relieved to see his old chum than he would admit.

'Nothing much,' Bullshot replied modestly.

'*Nothing much!*' repeated Rosemary, her face bathed in smiles and shining with admiration. 'You just saved the world from disaster!'

'Oh, top hole, Hugh!' cried Binky, really jolly pleased for his old pal.

But Hugh Crummond preferred action to words. 'Enough chatter, Binky,' he announced, climbing over to the driving seat. 'We have a race to win!'

Suddenly, with a roar, the open-tourer rally car accelerated past the car in front and tore off at a phenomenal speed.

In seconds it was a mere speck on the horizon.

34

THE RED DE HAVILLAND FOX MOTH was crossing the English coastline when the engine backfired with several coughs and a splutter. The needles of the gauges on the instrument panel spun wildly anti-clockwise as Count Otto von Brunno, muttering Teutonic curses, heaved on the controls and banged them with his fists.

But all that could be heard was the howling of the
wind as the plane careered downwards towards the
Channel. The one-time German flying ace glared
malevolently out of the cockpit, somehow convinced that
his arch-enemy Bullshot Crummond was standing on the
wing laughing at him as he plunged in the water. As
indeed, in a way, he was.

'I met him when I was a child,' murmured Lenya von
Brunno, her arm locked inside Professor Fenton's as she
sat beside him on the bed, her bosom pressing lightly
into the boffin's elbow.

'He poisoned my mind. I never meant to be evil.' She
sighed and moved even closer to the Professor, allowing
her hand to brush against his thigh. 'I only vanted to be

cared for.'

'Oh, I understand my dear,' Rupert Fenton replied sympathetically as Lenya cradled her head in his shoulder. 'I too know what it's like to be alone. You see...' he turned to her as to a mother confessor '... I blew up my wife...'

35

IN WHICH ROSEMARY GETS HER MAN, BINKY DOES HIS BIT AND BULLSHOT PULLS IT OFF

AS HUGH CRUMMOND in his open tourer, with Binky beside him and Rosemary in the back seat, roared across the finishing line of the London-to-Brighton Car Rally, the chequered flag waved and crowds of spectators cheered madly at the news that Bullshot had done it again.

'Bravo! Bravo!' shouted Rosemary, beside herself with joy, admiration and love for her hero.

Bullshot climbed into the back seat and stood with a wreath around his neck, one arm around the winning trophy, the other around Rosemary, to modestly acknowledge the cheers of all and sundry.

'I don't know how you do it, Crummond,' spluttered Binky. 'You changed the course of history and you still find time to win the London to Brighton!'

'Oh Hugh, you're wonderful!' sighed Rosemary.

'Not wonderful, Rosemary,' said Bullshot with stiff upper lip. 'Just British!'

And, with that, he gave her a whopping great kiss.

EPILOGUE

ON SUNDAY, 3 September 1932, along the road opposite the elm-lined churchyard of St Oswald's Parish Church, Horsted Keynes, Sussex, there marched a band of ex-servicemen buskers, a motley crew of four or five one-armed, one-legged, blind, deaf or dumb war-wounded veterans in threadbare uniforms bedecked with medals.

One played a concertina, another the trumpet; a third, wearing a red fez and striped nightgown, was floppily performing the Egyptian sand dance, another carried a sorry-looking flag and a big, battered bass drum that looked as though it had been run over by a bus and which bore the words 'Royal Loamshire Regiment' and the Latin inscription '*In Pace Semper Tedium Est*'. They suddenly interrupted their bittersweet butchery of patriotic songs and broke into the Wedding March.

As he sauntered out of the church on the arm of his blushing bride, Captain Hugh Crummond, in top hat and tails and sporting a white carnation, was thinking of his impending honeymoon and could hardly contain himself.

Here they all were – give or take a limb or two and a couple of those brave chaps who'd gone before – come to provide him with a guard of honour. It made a chap feel proud. With a tear of pride he sprang to attention.

'Look,' he yelled excitedly to Rosemary. 'There's some chaps from my old regiment, the Royal

Loamshires. Look—' he pointed '—there's Erskine ...
and Dusty Miller.'

Hands on hips, he regarded them fondly. You could
cut their arms and legs off, but they'd still be there,
singing and dancing like the troopers they would always
be.

'Did I ever tell you about the time I did a daisy cutter
in the old Camel?' he reminisced nostalgically, turning
back to Rosemary – but Mrs Hugh Crummond née
Fenton had at last abandoned all hope and was already
climbing awkwardly – because of her voluminous white
bridal outfit – into the ribbon-bedecked Rolls-Royce.

Torn between love and duty, Bullshot sighed
wretchedly. But the remains of his old regiment had
stopped playing and the one with the big bass drum was
giving him a salute with the flag.

'Captain Crummond,' he called out hoarsely, 'is it
really you? Let me shake you by the hand, sir.'

'Ah, Cunnington!' said Crummond jovially,
recognising him at once. 'How goes it, man?'

'No, sir. He's Dusty Miller,' replied Erskine.
'Cunningham, as you may recall, sir, fell in the line of
duty.'

So many brave chaps gone, thought Bullshot. For a
moment Miller hesitated to cross the road as he listened
for traffic. But Bullshot, filled with warmth and
bonhomie, would have none of it.

'Don't worry, laddie,' he called back cheerily, 'there's
no land mines in Horsted Keynes!'

Cautiously Miller started to cross the road, moving
awkwardly behind the drum, which, sadly, had no eyes
to see the festive-looking Rolls, cheered on by a crowd of
wellwishers, friends and relatives, back into him as it
lined itself up to depart.

'Come along, Crummond, old chap!' Binky called, already nervous about his Best Man speech. 'We'll be late for the reception!'

But the big bass drum was making a beeline for the groom and it bulldozed into him, sending him sprawling at the feet of his manservant.

'You mustn't keep the chauffeur waiting, sir,' said Dobbs as he helped him up and dusted him down. 'These foreign types can get rather shirty, and I'm sure Miss Fent— Mrs Crummond will be wanting you too, sir.'

'Don't worry, Dobbs,' Bullshot replied, climbing into the Rolls beside his bride and pulling out his pipe. 'I won't let the side down.'

As wellwishers threw their last handfuls of confetti, the Rolls took off, bound for London and the Ritz. Captain Crummond glared through the back window for a second at the ruffians across the road, and took Rosemary's hand in his.

'Full speed ahead,' he called cheerily to the chauffeur.

Outside the church, the wellwishers were going their separate ways or climbing into their cars for the reception. Soon only one was left and he was lying in the road, obviously overcome by the emotion of the ceremony. But the dazzling display had been lost on the ex-servicemen who stood in numbed silence, their hands covering the eyes of those who had not lost them in the trenches.

'Another good'un gone down,' said the newly

ordained Reverend Stanley Crouch, gazing with cherubic saintliness at his old comrade-in-arms in the trenches. 'Well, it's his funeral now, I suppose.'

'Absolutely, old boy,' replied Professor Sir Rupert Fenton. 'Still, I expect he'll make Rosemary a decent husband,' he sighed with joy and relief.

Fenton had recently been knighted for his work on super compressed particulate matter: he had finally solved the problem of Rosemary's scone mix. The Fenton Formula, the Hardest Substance Known to Man, now no longer went soggy in water, thanks to the addition of a single additional ingredient, following his soon-to-be son-in-law Hugh Crummond's accidental spillage into Rosemary's baking dish of a few flakes of Thomas & Blather's Extra Strong Pipe Tobacco.

The scones, already inedible, had instantly been rendered not only completely indestructible but highly inflammable, and thus at last constituted the awesome weapons of destruction that the late Count von Brunno had so keenly coveted.

Only a few days after Professor's investiture at Buckingham Palace, and a few weeks before the Crummond wedding, Reverend Crouch had officiated at another marriage, a discreet little ceremony in which Bullshot had performed his duties as best man immaculately.

'What a simply dazzling new wife you have, Professor,' said Bullshot.

'Isn't she, Crummond?' Fenton had replied proudly. 'But as you have agreed most heroically to take my daughter off my hands, I hope you will be so good as to call me Daddy.'

'Yes, of course, Professor … Daddy.'

'And as I will be your new mother, you must call me

ze Mummy,' purred the newly titled Lady Fenton – a most seductive-looking platinum blonde who, in a mere month, had undergone a truly remarkable transformation from grieving widow to blushing bride – as she devoured her new son-in-law maternally with her strangely familiar eyes.

'Yes, of course, Mrs ... Lady ... Mummy,' Bullshot stuttered.

'Your new stepmother has strangely familiar eyes, Rosemary,' Bullshot had whispered to Rosemary at the modest reception. 'Where might I have seen them before?'

'Daddy said she wescued him fwom that beastly von Bwunno, but he wefused to elabowate,' Rosemary had whispered back.

Basking in the hazy aftermath of his daughter's wedding, Professor Fenton gazed with pleasure as the happy couple's Rolls receded into the distance.

'Interesting chauffeur,' he remarked to Reverend Crouch. 'I was chatting to him about an old theory of mine, the general one on Relativity. I wrote a note about it some time ago – 1904, I think – but I can't think what I did with it. I do hope it didn't get into the hands of my German rival, though it's more likely, I suspect, that the dog swallowed it...

'In any case, this chauffeur chappie seemed far more interested in my new formula for splitting the hydrogen atom. I haven't worked out the ramifications or applications, but he showed a keen appreciation and he even seemed to think it could help control planets…'

In the back seat of the Rolls, Crummond was trying unsuccessfully to get his pipe going. There was something not quite right about the Thomas & Blather's tobacco. Was it his imagination or did it have just the tiniest suggestion of the fermented, acidic aroma of sauerkraut?

Suddenly he ceased his fumblings as he noticed in the driving mirror the crescent-faced chauffeur leering at him and Rosemary in the most familiar way.

Bullshot pulled down the blind. At the driving wheel Count Otto von Brunno fumed, accelerated, and turned off the main road in the direction of Netherington Manor.

He still had the diamonds, he consoled himself. Synthetic diamonds are forever.

But all that, of course, is another story…

About the Authors

Martin Noble is a writer, editor and publisher, based in Oxford. His novel adaptations include: *Bullshot, Private Schulz, Ruthless People, Tin Men, Bloodbath at the House of Death, One Magic Christmas, Automan, Cover Up* and *Who Framed Roger Rabbit.* His novels include *Trance Mission.*

Diz White is an actress, comedy writer and director. Diz starred as Rosemary Fenton in the 1983 movie *Bullshot* and also starred in *Too Much Oregano*, winner of the Best Short award at the Cannes Film Festival. Her plays include: *El Grande de Coca-Cola, Bullshot Crummond* and *Footlight Frenzy.* Her books include: *Cotswold Memoir, Haunted Cheltenham, Haunted Cotswolds* and *The Comedy Group Book.*

Ron House founded Low Moan Spectacular, the London underground theatre company, with whom he created the hits *Bullshot Crummond* and *El Grande de Coca-Cola* (London, New York, Los Angeles and San Francisco). Ron has five published plays with three more waiting. His latest work, *Decorum Maintained,* was inspired by personal experiences working as an under butler in the London townhouse of Klaus and Sonny Von Bulow.

Alan Shearman is a founder member of Low Moan Spectacular, the British comedy group with whom he created *El Grande de Coca-Cola, Footlight Frenzy* and *Bullshot Crummond.* He works regularly as a voice actor on what now totals several hundred movies, TV shows and video games. He has also written screenplays for several comedy movies and action-adventure TV miniseries and is a six-time award-winning stage director. http://lowmoan.com/ashearman/index.html

Lightning Source UK Ltd.
Milton Keynes UK
UKOW02f2327241116
288515UK00001B/77/P